CENTURION

GALACTIC GLADIATORS: HOUSE OF RONE #3

ANNA HACKETT

Centurion

Published by Anna Hackett

Copyright 2019 by Anna Hackett

Cover by Melody Simmons of BookCoversCre8tive

Cover image by Paul Henry Serres

Edits by Tanya Saari

ISBN (ebook): 978-1-925539-84-4

ISBN (paperback): 978-1-925539-85-1

The Phoenix Adventures – SFR Galaxy Award Winner for Most Fun New Series and "Why Isn't This a Movie?" Series

Beneath a Trojan Moon – SFR Galaxy Award Winner and RWAus Ella Award Winner

Hell Squad – SFR Galaxy Award for best Post-Apocalypse for Readers who don't like Post-Apocalypse

"Like Indiana Jones meets Star Wars. A treasure hunt with a steamy romance." – SFF Dragon, review of *Among Galactic Ruins*

"Strap in, enjoy the heat of romance and the daring of this group of space travellers!" – Di, Top 500 Amazon Reviewer, review of *At Star's End*

"Action, danger, aliens, romance – yup, it's another great book from Anna Hackett!" – Book Gannet Reviews, review of *Hell Squad: Marcus*

Sign up for my VIP mailing list and get your *free box set* containing three action-packed romances.

Visit here to get started:
www.annahackettbooks.com

CHAPTER ONE

He sprinted down the tunnel, using every bit of his enhanced speed.

At a junction, Acton Vonn stopped. He was in the old, rock-cut tunnels of the abandoned fight rings, deep beneath the city of Kor Magna.

He tilted his head and used his cyborg hearing. *There.* He detected harsh breathing and running foot-steps. Breaking into a sprint again, he followed the sound.

He turned a corner and came out in an open area where tiered seating was cut into the rock walls. This training arena had once been used by the Thraxians. The aliens had abducted people from all around the galaxy and forced them to fight to the death in these rings for the amusement of anyone who paid the price for entry.

Thankfully, the House of Galen put a stop to that.

"Acton, the target took another side tunnel. East of your current location."

The smooth voice of Jaxer Rone—second of the

1

House of Rone—echoed through Acton's built-in comm system.

"Acknowledged." Acton turned, pumping his cybernetic arms and using more of his enhanced speed. Soon, he sensed the man—his racing pulse, his labored breathing, his stumbled steps. Stats flickered up in front of Acton's left eye. With another burst of speed, he darted down the tunnel and spotted his prey.

In a rush of power, Acton pinned the man to the wall.

"Don't kill me!"

The man's robes were dirty and disheveled. Unfortunately, Acton's enhanced senses got a full hit of the man's awful, unwashed smell. "I won't need to kill you if you answer my questions."

At Acton's cold tone, the man whimpered. "P-please."

"I'm a cyborg. I don't feel anything, so pleading is useless."

The man ran his shaking hand across his mouth. "You're a monster."

Acton had heard variations of that before. Half his face was made of metal, both his arms were cybernetic. People preferred to be afraid and see monster instead of man. Since his emotional dampeners kept him from feeling, he didn't care.

"Now, Darga—"

"You know my name." The man trembled.

"We know everything about you." A man who stole and sold anything and everything. "The humans who were taken by the Edull. Tell us what you know of them."

Darga's eyelids flickered. "I-I don't know anything."

Acton put more pressure on the man's neck.

"Nothing!" The terrified man's voice rose. "I know nothing."

Acton kept up the pressure until Darga started to choke.

"Acton," a deep voice said.

He'd already heard the scrape of boots behind him. Jax stepped forward, his red cloak resting down his back. The other cyborg was as tall as Acton, with a muscled body and a dash of silver along one cheekbone. His bare chest and arms showed off the intricate tattoo on his right arm, which was also a deadly weapon. His cybernetic leg was hidden under his fighting leathers.

Two more shadows appeared out of the gloom of the tunnels. One was larger, with a huge, muscled chest and wide shoulders. Mace. The other cyborg was leaner, a weapon rising up out of the implant on his shoulder, and his blonde hair loose around his face. Toren. They were all part of the House of Rone's elite fighters.

"This man is lying," Acton said coolly.

"I know," Jax replied. "But don't kill him yet."

Darga whimpered again.

Acton thought of Quinn, Jayna, Calla, and Sage. Three women from Earth, and one from the planet Rella. They'd all been abducted by alien slavers and sold to the Edull. Ripped from their lives and locked in cages and labs. The metal-scavenging Edull had kept the women in the desert, imprisoned them, tortured them.

Detailed memories of when he'd rescued Sage moved

through his head. When he'd first seen her, she'd been floating in a lab tank, her copper-colored hair like a cloud around her small body. The Edull had been experimenting on her.

His gaze sharpened on the man in front of him. When his cybernetic eye glowed, he saw Darga swallow. From intel the House of Rone had gathered, they knew that this rat worked for the Edull. Those women had been innocent, and the Edull had had no right to prey on them.

Sage was free of the lab now, and she and Acton had become friends. She smiled a lot, but even Acton, with his limited understanding of emotions, wondered if she was really okay.

"The Edull are beyond angry at the House of Rone," Darga burst out angrily. "You tin heads better be ready. They're planning their revenge."

"How?" Acton demanded.

"I don't know." An ugly smile crossed his lips, showcasing rotting teeth that had been sharpened to points. "But there's trouble coming."

Acton released the man and stepped back. As he stepped away from the wall, Darga rubbed his neck. Acton raised his hands. Then the man's body rose up into the air, his feet lifting off the ground. Energy throbbed along Acton's cybernetic arms as he used his abilities. He could manipulate energy to lift and move objects.

Darga kicked his arms and legs. "Let me go!"

"The humans," Acton said again.

"I don't *know*. They have some at Bari Batu. That's all I know."

The Edull's hidden city in the desert.

"And where is Bari Batu?" Jax asked.

"I've never been there. I don't know!"

Acton increased his kinetic power and lifted Darga higher. Then the man started to choke.

"Acton," Jax said in a warning tone.

Acton dropped the man and Darga hit the rock floor. As the rat continued to gasp and wheeze, Acton frowned. "It's not me causing him to choke."

The man started convulsing, blood pouring out of his nose.

"*Drak.*" Jax gripped Darga's head, touching the man's face. A small implant was visible up one nostril. "An Edull implant."

"*Drakking* sandsuckers," Mace muttered.

An implant to ensure the man didn't share any secrets. Acton eyed the dying man dispassionately. He was no great loss.

Finally, Darga stopped moving, and Acton no longer detected any life signs.

Mace let out an angry growl, and Toren shook his head.

Jax cursed and kicked the wall in a display of emotion. Jax had always felt more than the rest of them, and now that he was mated to Quinn, the man was more prone to smiling, and other emotional responses.

"What?" Acton asked.

"Now I have to tell Quinn that we have no leads." Jax set his hands on his hips. "I hate upsetting her and the others. They really want to find the other captive humans."

Jax and Quinn had fallen in love. Although, it all started with their imperator, Magnus Rone. The powerful cyborg had fallen in love with Ever, one of the human survivors from the Fortuna Space Station. Jax had followed after he'd rescued the fierce Quinn from the desert. And now, even Mace shared his quarters with Jayna.

His fellow cyborgs were falling in love all around him, and Acton still didn't quite understand any of it. Particularly, all these emotions.

"Let's get out of here," Jax said.

The cyborgs headed out of the maze of dark tunnels. Acton could tell Jax and Mace were eager to get back to their women, and he shook his head.

He didn't feel anything. Once, as a boy, he had, but that time was such a vague, distant memory it was almost forgotten.

The Metathim military had altered him, changed him. And now there was no man left to feel.

SHE WAS SURROUNDED BY SMILING, laughing women.

And she'd never felt more alone in her life.

Sage McAlister watched Ever Haynes pick up her baby. The little girl, Asha, giggled, her chubby fingers gripping her mother's dark hair.

Quinn, the former security chief of the *Helios*, was standing nearby, nodding at Jayna. The athletic woman stood straight, wearing fitted, leather trousers and a tank top. Her blonde-brown hair was braided. Jayna was smiling, her dark hair loose, as she ate a dessert from the tray of delicious things on the table. They'd all been made by Calla, their alien friend, who was currently busy in the kitchen, crafting more tasty creations.

Sage felt like an island of quiet—disconnected and remote.

"Sage? Sage?"

She blinked and looked up to find all the women staring at her.

"Sorry." She pasted on a wide smile. "My mind wandered. What did I miss?"

Concern crossed Ever's face, and she hitched her baby higher on her hip. "Are you okay?"

"Fabulous." Sage was free, alive. She *should* be on top of the world. But inside she felt the heavy beat of dark memories. Just thinking of her time with the Edull made her shiver.

You're free, you should be happy and grateful.

It certainly didn't help that they could never return home to Earth. Ever. When the Thraxian slavers had attacked the *Helios* exploration ship, they'd used a transient wormhole to reach Earth's solar system. That wormhole was long gone. Now, for better or worse, the desert world of Carthago was home.

Then, there were her memories of enslavement under the Edull. Her fingers flexed. Horrifying, nightmarish memories. She refused to think of those right now.

After a beat, the women started talking again. Quinn was discussing training with the cyborgs and gladiators who called the House of Rone home. Ever and Jayna were comparing notes about their work in Ever's lab.

They had a good place here, Sage reminded herself. They'd been rescued by the House of Rone, and offered sanctuary. It was more than most would get.

So why did Sage still feel chilled?

She rubbed her cold hands together. She didn't want to tell the other women. They'd all done so much to make her feel welcome here, to feel safe.

There was an echo of noise and deep voices outside in the hall.

Quinn jumped up. "The boys are back."

Sage stifled a brief chuckle. The *boys* were actually a group of lethal cyborgs, the elite of the House of Rone. They were the least boy-like men Sage had ever seen.

The women moved out the door into the hall, and Sage followed. She watched Quinn move straight to Jax, the man's cloak snapping as he wrapped an arm around his woman and hugged her close.

Mace followed suit, engulfing Jayna in his brawny arms. Toren and Acton were standing nearby. Toren nodded, but her gaze snagged on Acton.

His ice-blue eyes lifted to meet hers, and he gave her a small nod. The light in the corridor glinted off the metal on his arms and face. Both his arms were cybernetic, and she knew they housed deadly weapons. Half his face was metal as well, and it kept people from noticing the other side of his face. He was really quite handsome, with a strong jaw and straight nose. His hair was deep brown and cut short. His skin was a gorgeous, golden shade.

But no emotion showed on that attractive face.

So emotionless, so cold, so powerful. She'd spent a fair bit of time with him during her recovery. She found it easy to be with Acton. With him, she didn't have to pretend to be happy all the time.

But she had to remind herself, Acton was a weapon—honed to the most lethal edge.

"How did it go?" Quinn asked.

Jax heaved out a breath, his handsome face troubled. "Badly. The informant didn't know anything, and then the Edull implant he had killed him."

Ever drew in a sharp breath, pulling Asha closer.

Mace scowled. "He did tell us that the Edull are planning to cause trouble for the House of Rone."

The women all gasped.

"Fuckers," Quinn muttered, her face fierce.

The thud of heavy footsteps sounded. They all swiveled as a large figure headed toward them down the corridor.

Imperator Magnus Rone sure made an impact.

Sage took in the man's hard face, big, strong body, and foreboding features. But as his gaze hit his mate and daughter, something crossed his expression, softening it.

This was the cyborg who'd escaped a harsh military cyborg program, and started the House of Rone. Now, the house was known for some of the best gladiators to fight in the Kor Magna Arena, the best weapons, and their skill with cybernetic enhancements.

"We'll keep searching for your fellow humans," Magnus said. "We *will* find Bari Batu, and put a stop to the Edull's slavery."

Sage's throat closed. There were other humans out

there. Other crew members from the *Helios* who were trapped, afraid, in pain.

She sensed someone move closer. When she looked up, she saw Acton watching her carefully. She'd been teaching him to read small cues as to how people were feeling. Right now, she wished she was invisible.

"The informant didn't give us any leads," Jax told Magnus. "Except to let us know that the Edull are planning to cause us trouble."

Magnus' face didn't change, but Sage felt a chill go down her spine.

"They can try," Magnus said.

"We'll make them regret it," Mace added.

"Sage," Magnus said. "Avarn tells me that you've been helping in Medical, but that you haven't officially joined the healers."

She felt everyone look at her and her chest tightened. "Yes."

"He was impressed by your skills."

It felt like Magnus' gaze could see right through her skin. Her stomach churned. "Avarn's been great, but I'm not...ready yet."

There were sympathetic nods all around, and Ever touched Sage's arm. "There's no rush. Take your time. You're still recovering and settling in."

Finally, everyone's attention shifted elsewhere, and Sage let out a shaky breath.

As they all started talking, making plans for the next steps on what to do to find Bari Batu, Acton stepped closer to her.

"Sage, you're well?"

That cool, controlled voice made her want to smile. "I'm fine, Acton."

"Ever is correct. There is no need for you to rush into work."

"I know." She slid a strand of hair behind her ear. The thing was, she wanted to be productive and useful. She wanted to contribute to her new home. Still, the thought of doing her paramedic work paralyzed her, for some reason. She'd loved being a paramedic aboard the *Helios*, but now...she felt adrift.

She hadn't been able to help anyone during the attack or while she'd been imprisoned by the Edull. She hadn't even been able to help herself.

The faintest frown touched Acton's face. "You are not fine."

"How can you tell?" she asked.

"Your downcast mouth and eyes. Your tense shoulders."

She took a deep breath. "You've been listening to me."

When she'd first arrived, they'd agreed to be friends. Over the last few weeks, he'd taught her about the city of Kor Magna, and life on the desert world of Carthago. In return, she'd been teaching him about emotions.

"What's wrong?" he asked quietly.

She glanced at the others to make sure no one was listening. She kept her voice low. "I don't know. Sometimes I just want to scream." She shrugged. "Everything just closes in on me, sometimes. I..."

She *should* be grateful. She *should* be happy. Suddenly, she needed some space.

"I need to go."

"Sage—"

She shook her head, and before anyone else noticed her, she hurried off down the corridor. She wasn't sure where she was going, but she needed air.

CHAPTER TWO

Acton watched Sage disappear down the corridor.
Quinn's curse made him turn back to the group.

The tall woman's face was twisted. She was clearly angry.

"We have no leads." Quinn's voice was as sharp as a blade. "Nothing. No way to find Bari Batu."

In recent days, they'd run several flights near the outpost where they'd rescued Sage and Calla, but there was no sign of the desert scrap city or the Edull.

Quinn ground her teeth together and Acton watched curiously. So much emotion that he didn't understand.

He turned his head, looking down the empty hallway in the direction where Sage had gone.

She didn't show as much of her feelings, or at least, not her true feelings. Some part of him understood enough to know that Sage wasn't happy. And that she was hiding it.

He frowned, uncertain why that fact bothered him, but it did.

"We'll keep searching, Quinn," Magnus said. "I have a meeting with the House of Galen tomorrow. And Zhim and Ryan, along with Rillian and Corsair, are all doing whatever they can to track down the city's location."

Zhim and Ryan were information merchants, and Rillian and Corsair were powerful allies. Ryan was from Earth and now mated with Zhim. They had all helped rescue the Fortuna Space Station survivors, and were now helping find the humans taken from the *Helios*.

"I suggest we plan another desert recon mission," Jax said.

Magnus nodded. "Do it."

As his fellow cyborgs dispersed, Mace lifted his chin at Acton. "Want to hit the gym for some training?"

"No, I have an errand to attend to," Acton said.

He headed down the corridor, and found himself at the House of Rone kitchens. Inside, there was a hubbub of noise and movement. The team of chefs were busy preparing meals for everyone who called the House of Rone home.

The head chef lifted his head and frowned. He was D'nonian with patterned skin that almost looked like the pelt of a cat.

"Acton?" The man's eyebrows rose. "I don't see you in here...well, ever."

Acton had no reason to come and talk to the chef. He ate the nutritionally balanced meals that the chef and his team made for the cyborgs. Food was simply fuel to Acton, that was it.

"I'd like to request some *panella*."

The chef's eyebrows rose even more. "For you?"

"No." He knew that Sage loved the sweet treats. He'd seen her popping them in her mouth on numerous occasions. They had a very high sugar content.

With a shrug, the chef moved to a cupboard, opened some doors, and came back and handed Acton a small bag of the round, blue treats.

"Thank you," Acton said.

As he headed out of the kitchens, he suspected he knew where Sage was. He checked her room first, but found it empty. The scent of her was strong in the room—sweet and light.

He swiveled, then headed back through the stone-lined corridors covered in wall hangings of deep blue. They all depicted gladiators fighting in the arena. He moved up two sets of stairs.

When he stepped out onto the rooftop, he saw that Carthago's dual suns were setting. Bright, golden light bathed the city.

The rooftop didn't get used a lot, but there was a small seating area with low cushions, and with shade cloths strung up above it. They fluttered quietly in the breeze.

Sage's copper-colored hair glinted in the sunlight. She sat there, her knees curled up to her chest and her chin resting on top.

She didn't hear him approach.

"Sage?"

She jumped. "*God*. You scared me."

"That was not my intention."

Acton leaned against the railing. Up here, he had a very good view of Kor Magna. It was mostly low, two-

and three-story buildings made from the local cream stone. To the left, the ancient walls of the Kor Magna arena rose up, and to the right, the towering, glowing spears of the glitzy buildings of the District.

Out of habit, he scanned the area for anything untoward.

"What are you doing?" Sage asked.

He glanced over his shoulder and saw she was watching him.

"Assessing for threats."

"Why?"

"It's what I do."

"Oh."

He let his gaze catalog the features of her face. "You're upset. I wanted to ensure that you were all right."

She sighed. "I want to be all right."

Acton felt a strange tug in his stomach and frowned at the sensation. "You suffered a terrible experience, Sage. It takes time to recover. That's a normal reaction."

"I'm safe, and others aren't." She huffed out a breath.

"You feel guilt."

"I feel everything sometimes. Guilt, sadness, fear, anger." She shoved her hands into her hair. "But most of the time, I feel nothing. Everyone has done so much for me..."

Drawn by her, he knelt down on the cushions beside her. Her eyes—a fascinating mix of brown and green—met his.

"No one expects anything in return. From my observations, your fellow humans don't want anything from you. They just want you to be happy."

"Acton, I feel empty and cold inside." Her words were barely more than a whisper.

Should he touch her? He wasn't sure. He'd seen Magnus, Jax, and Mace touch their women to comfort them. His metal fingers often repulsed people though. As much as he felt the urge to reach for her, he held himself back.

"The sense of disconnection is normal, Sage. It will fade."

"Is that how you feel all the time? Cold? empty?" Her big eyes locked on his face.

"I feel glimmers of sensation. I don't feel the highs and lows of emotion. Lately, I get a lot of bemusement and confusion."

That earned him a faint smile. "All these chaotic humans around you?"

"Yes."

"Poor cyborg."

She was teasing him? No one teased him. "Give yourself time, Sage. You're still recovering. Don't worry about how you feel today, because I am certain it will change over the coming days and weeks."

"You're giving me advice about emotions," she said.

"It appears I am. Perhaps you should talk to Ever or Quinn—"

"No." She shook her head quickly. "I like talking with you. You're cool, pragmatic."

Perhaps that's what Sage needed. He pulled the small bag from his pocket. "I have something for you."

He handed her the *panella*.

She held up the clear bag and her eyes widened. She opened the packet and smiled.

"Oh, I love these." She popped one small sweet into her mouth and made a humming noise.

Watching her savor the sweetness, Acton felt a strange tensing in his gut.

"Thank you, Acton." She pressed a hand against one of his, her fingers brushing the metal. "I know you say you don't feel, but I don't buy it."

He cleared his throat. "Sage—"

"You are way too nice not to feel anything. But don't worry—" she bumped her shoulder against his "—your secret is safe with me."

THE NEXT MORNING, Sage walked down a set of steps in the House of Rone, her steps light.

She felt a little better and she'd slept surprisingly well. Her quiet time with Acton and bingeing on *panella* had helped.

Today, she was *not* going to beat herself up about not feeling on top of the world. As a paramedic, she'd been practical and focused. As a woman, she liked to believe the best in people. She hated negativity of any kind. But the Edull had drained some of that positivity out of her.

How she was feeling right now was normal. *Give yourself time.* Acton's cool voice slid through her head.

She smiled. Of everyone around her on this strange alien planet, the lethal, emotionless cyborg made her feel the most confident and secure. She shook her head.

The sound of fighting from the training arena filled the air. At the bottom of the stairs, she turned a corner, and then paused.

The arena had a sand floor, and was currently dotted with mostly shirtless gladiators and cyborgs. There were a few females, but not many. They were mostly males—big, muscled males.

Not a bad view, she had to admit.

Several of the gladiators were unenhanced. Ever had told her that cyborgs were banned from fighting in the famous gladiatorial arena, so their fighters had to be devoid of enhancements. She spotted Xias—the champion of the House of Rone gladiators. His dark skin was slicked with sweat. He swung a giant axe, roaring as it smacked into a training dummy.

She saw two younger, leaner cyborgs training together. One had a metal leg that was streamlined and futuristic. Another had several circular implants across his body.

Their swords clashed violently, and they were both breathing heavily.

"Stop." A familiar voice.

Acton stepped into view. Black, leather trousers hugged his long, toned legs, and he wasn't wearing a shirt.

The sunlight glinted off his metal arms, and the rest of his skin was that glorious shade of gold. Her gaze drifted downward, over a toned, tight stomach. He was leaner than Mace and Magnus, all honed strength. She watched him patiently explain something to the young cyborgs.

They both nodded, listening intently. Acton lifted a sword, his muscles flexing.

Sage's mouth went dry, and she felt a flicker of desire.

Crap. Her mouth dropped open. This was *Acton*. He was her friend. He was a cyborg who didn't feel, or rather, he did, but it was very muted. What he did feel, he liked to ignore.

Then she watched him move.

He launched into the fight sequence, moving like a blur. He spun, his body agile, the swing of the sword smooth and powerful.

Sage felt herself go damp between her legs.

Oh, God. She was lusting after Acton. This wasn't good.

She backed up a few steps, her hip hitting the wall.

All of a sudden, he stopped, and lifted his head. Across the sand, his gaze zeroed in on her. He didn't smile, but he lifted a hand.

Heart pounding in her chest, she waved back.

Then she turned and quickly walked away. She didn't want him to talk to her right now. Jayna had told her that the cyborgs all had enhanced senses. They could smell a woman's arousal.

Crapola. Don't be stupid, Sage.

Acton didn't feel. Of all the people for her to be attracted to... Her mother had liked to tell Sage—repeatedly—that men were no-good users. Some of her earliest memories were of her mother's "friends" dropping by. Her mom would set Sage in front of the television and disappear into her room with her man of the moment. They never lasted long.

She spotted the drinks table set up for the exercising gladiators. She grabbed some water and gulped it down. She knew her mother was a bitter woman who blamed other people for her own failings. There were plenty of nice, affectionate guys out there.

Acton just wasn't one of them.

This was silly. She closed her eyes. It would pass.

She'd had several nice boyfriends, and she'd liked sex. She pulled a face. Although, after thinking she was dead, Daniel had happily moved on with somebody else and was now expecting a baby. Sage had to admit that stung a bit.

She'd always, always wanted someone who loved her. When she was younger, she'd dreamed of a prince or a knight, who'd sweep her away, and love and protect her. As she got older, she'd just wanted a man who put her first and loved her completely. Her mother never had, and Daniel never had.

That was something she could never have with Acton.

Hearing a feminine giggle, she looked up.

She spotted Calla and Zaden. The cyborg had the alien woman pressed against the stone wall, stealing a kiss.

She watched him raise his head, then he smiled at the pretty, brown-skinned Calla. Sage froze. Zaden had been so cool and composed just weeks ago. Power literally thrummed from him. She never could have imagined him smiling like this, love in his eyes.

But Calla had woken something up in the powerful

cyborg. When she'd been in danger, he'd done everything to save her.

Could Acton wake up and embrace his emotions too? Sage bit her lip. He was way more enhanced than the others.

"Sage?"

Ever's voice made Sage jolt. "Oh, hi."

"Are you all right?" The woman's pale-green gaze narrowed.

Sage pulled out her *I'm fine* smile. "I'm great. Where's Asha?"

"With her daddy."

Magnus Rone toting his tiny daughter around... Maybe miracles did happen.

"Hey," Ever said. "I have a favor to ask."

"Sure."

"I usually teach a class today with several of the House of Rone kids. I teach them about Earth, the different animals, peoples, customs. But I have some people coming in to take a look at some tech that I've been working on in the lab. Jayna's going to be with me, and I'm not sure how Quinn would do with a room full of kids." Ever's nose wrinkled. "She'd probably teach them to throw a punch or swing a staff. Could you help me out?"

"Sounds like fun." Sage nodded, happy to be helpful in some small way. "Sure thing."

Ever smiled. "You're a lifesaver, Sage."

CHAPTER THREE

S age walked into the bright, airy room, and a bunch of curious faces turned to look up at her.

She was just as curious about them. All the children in the room were of different alien species. Mostly humanoid—thanks to the ancient aliens she'd learned had seeded life throughout the galaxy—but there was still a mix of different-colored skin, interesting patterns, and some with cybernetic enhancements.

"Hi, I'm Sage." She smiled brightly.

She got waves, hellos, and shy smiles.

"You were rescued," one confident boy with dark skin said.

"Yes."

"Were there explosions during your rescue?" a girl asked. "Did you see the cyborgs fight?"

Sage smiled. Kids were apparently the same whatever planet they came from. "Sorry, I was mostly unconscious at the time."

"I'm glad you're safe." A wide-eyed boy shot her a sweet smile.

"Thanks, me too."

A pretty girl with dark hair and a gold pattern along the edges of her face leaned forward. "I was rescued too."

Sage smiled at Nemma. The little alien girl came from Rella, the same planet as Calla.

"I know. I'm glad that you're safe, Nemma."

From what Sage had heard, the girl was settling in well at the House of Rone. Despite being wrenched from her family and dragged away by alien slavers, she'd bounced back. She'd been placed with the family of one of the House of Rone workers who had other children her age. But Sage knew the young girl spent a lot of time with Calla and Zaden as well.

Leaning against the desk at the front of the room, Sage set her hands on the smooth surface. "So, I'm here to talk to you about Earth."

Ever had some pictures up on the screen and Sage pointed. "This is my planet."

There were gasps all around.

"So much water!" an older boy said.

"That's right. It has lots of different climates, from icy poles at the very north and the south, to mountains, forests, jungles, and deserts like Carthago. Years ago, our climate was changing due to increasing population, and people not taking care of the environment as much as they could. But clever humans used their brains, and they managed our resources well and invented better technology to help us recycle, create cleaner energy, and keep our oceans clean."

"Where are you from on Earth?" an older girl asked.

"A place called Austin, Texas." Sage pointed at a map. "About here."

A boy propped his chin on his cupped palm. "Is your family still there?"

"My mother is."

"What about your father? Or don't you have one?"

"My father wasn't around."

Nemma nibbled on her bottom lip. "Your mother must miss you."

There was such sadness in the little girl's voice, and it stabbed at Sage. Unfortunately, Sage's mother was a disinterested parent. Jenny McAlister had accidentally fallen pregnant young, and Sage's father had taken off. Her mother had always seen her child as a burden. Sage had tried so hard, for so long, to be a good daughter. She'd wanted a good relationship with the woman who'd given birth to her, wanted love and affection. It'd taken years before Sage had finally given up.

With a tight smile, she made a noncommittal sound. "Okay, let's talk about animals."

One boy clapped his hands. "Do you have *tarnids*?"

"Or vicious desert night beasts?" another child called out.

Sage laughed. "No." Instead she talked about elephants, giraffes, lions, crocodiles, kangaroos, and different species of birds.

The kids' expressions and comments made her smile. They were so energetic and enthusiastic, and it was hard not to feel good around them.

25

There was a knock at the door and she looked up. As Acton entered, all the kids' eyes went wide.

Damn, all that shirtless, golden skin made her mouth go dry.

"Sage." He gave her a nod.

She cleared her throat. "Acton. Did you need something?"

A groove appeared on his brow. "Just to see you."

The words made Sage feel warm inside. She knew he didn't mean them that way, but then she realized that he was checking on her, and in his own way, he did care.

She smiled at him. He looked so cool and remote, and he expected nothing from her. That made her relax.

"Acton, what planet are you from?" she asked.

"Tiarla. A farming world."

Sage blinked. Acton, a farmer? She could *not* picture that.

"How did you end up a cyborg?" one curious child asked.

Acton turned. "I was taken from my home by the Metathim and forced into a military program."

His voice was emotionless, but Sage's belly curdled. A tiny tick appeared beside his eye. It was all too easy to imagine a young, terrified boy ripped away from his family.

"Okay." Sage clapped her hands and turned back to the children. "Does anyone have any questions about Earth?"

"Does everyone on Earth look like you, Sage?" a girl asked.

"No!" a boy cried. "Ever's from Earth, and she has darker hair and darker skin than Sage."

"Jayna too," a girl said. "Plus, she has beautiful curls."

"And Quinn has gold hair and is much taller."

"Yes, and Sage is short," Nemma added.

Sage laughed. "Thanks, you guys. No, all humans can look very different, but for all our differences, we're the same on the inside." She moved over to the map, scrolling through to the one she wanted.

"Here." She touched the continent of Africa. "Many people who live here have darker skin and dark hair." She dragged her finger upward. "Around here, people tend to have paler skin and paler hair. And over here." She moved across Asia. "People can have brown skin, while over here they often have black hair, paler skin, and eyes that are tilted at the edges. People on Earth come in lots of different shapes and sizes."

Suddenly, Nemma gasped. The little girl's brown skin paled, leaving the golden pattern on her cheeks in stark relief.

Sage frowned and flicked a glance at Acton. He was staring at the child.

"Nemma?" Sage asked cautiously. "Are you okay?"

The girl shook her head. Acton pushed away from the wall. "Can you tell us what's distressing you?"

Sage crouched beside the girl. Nemma's dark pupils were dilated, her breathing fast.

"You can tell me," Sage said quietly.

"I saw a girl." Nemma licked her lips. "Like you described. Pale skin, straight, black hair, and dark eyes that tilted up."

Sage felt like the air had been sucked out of her and her belly clenched tight.

Nemma pressed a fist to her chest. "She was kept by the Edull, just like me."

Oh, God. "Do you know her name?"

"Grace. Her name was Grace."

Sage swiveled and looked at Acton. He held out a cybernetic hand to her. "The lesson is over. We need to talk to Magnus."

ACTON STOOD behind Sage in Ever's sitting room. The young girl, Nemma, sat in a chair beside her, fidgeting. He knew enough now to know the girl was nervous.

But Sage held her hand, and murmured to her in a warm, calm voice.

His eyes narrowed on Sage. She looked the most relaxed he'd seen her, and he realized that helping the little girl soothed her.

Ever stood nearby, face serious, leaning against a table. No one was calmed by the airy room and comfortable couches.

Then Magnus, Jax, and Quinn entered. The imperator strode over to his mate, and gently touched her face.

"Asha?" Ever asked.

"With Jayna," Magnus responded.

"Hey, Nems." Quinn smiled at the girl.

Nemma managed a small smile. "Hi, Quinn."

"Sage said you have something to tell us." Quinn moved closer. "About a human girl."

Nemma nodded.

Acton knew that they hadn't pushed the girl about her captivity. The healers had wanted her fully recovered before anyone asked her too many tough questions about her time at Bari Batu.

"I saw a girl. Grace. She was a little bigger than me and she looked Asian. Sage was telling us about different people on Earth and how they looked different on the outside."

Magnus' face turned grim, and Jax and Quinn traded a look.

Quinn shifted closer, bending down beside Nemma's chair. "There was a scientist aboard the *Helios*. Dr. Simone Li. She was one of the few crew members who had family with her. Her eight-year-old daughter...Grace."

"*Drak*," Jax muttered.

Nemma's bottom lip trembled and Acton catalogued the movement. Another sign of distress.

"Where did you see Grace, Nemma?" Sage asked.

"She was kept in a cell, like me."

The thought of this child in a cell caused a spike of emotion against Acton's emotional dampeners. The Edull were the worst sandsuckers.

For a brief second, he had a flash of a very old memory. Of a cold, empty cell that he'd been thrust into. Bright lights, screams, his own beating heart.

Acton frowned. His memories from his own abduction were little more than a faded blur.

"Sometimes the bad aliens let us out together, to exercise," Nemma said. "That's when I saw her."

"Okay, that's great, Nemma." Sage patted the little girl's shoulder.

"I spoke to her once. She was...fierce. She said she was going to escape and rescue her mother."

They all froze.

"Did she say that she'd seen her mother?" Quinn asked.

Nemma nodded.

"Where did they take you to exercise?" Magnus asked.

"Mostly, in a yard." Nemma's nose wrinkled. "It wasn't much fun." Then the girl's face brightened. "Once, they took us to the lake and we splashed in the water."

Acton frowned. He saw similar expressions on Magnus and Jax. Carthago was a desert planet.

"Lake?" Magnus said carefully.

Nemma nodded, playing with the hem of her skirt. "We swam and splashed, but I'm not a good swimmer, so I didn't go in far. The lake was huge, and I couldn't see the other side."

"Thank you, Nemma," Sage said. "You've been very helpful."

"Grace and the others shouldn't be stuck out there." Nemma's dark, pleading eyes took them all in. "They shouldn't be left alone and scared. I want them to be happy, like I am now."

Acton watched Sage reach out and hug the girl. Then Ever stepped forward. "Nemma, let's see if chef is willing to get us some ice cream." She held out a hand.

Nemma happily left with the woman.

Jax pressed a hand to his hip. "There are no lakes in Carthago's deserts."

"Could it have been an oasis?" Quinn suggested.

Magnus shook his head. "I've never heard of an oasis where you couldn't see the other side."

Acton frowned. "Hologram?"

"Holograms require a lot of energy to power," Magnus said. "I can't see the Edull wasting vast amounts of energy to entertain captive children."

"Assholes," Sage said. "Keeping kids prisoner."

"They'll pay," Quinn said with a growl, her voice ripe with promise.

"What now?" Sage asked.

"We talk with all our contacts and informants," Magnus said. "Nemma gave us new pieces of information today. Grace and Simone Li have been confirmed to have been at Bari Batu. And the Edull city is close to a lake."

"We find this lake, then we find Simone and Grace," Quinn said.

But a heavy pall settled on the room, and even Acton knew why. There were no lakes in the desert.

He looked at Sage and saw her hands twisted together. He thought about touching her, to offer comfort, but he wasn't exactly sure how. Instead, he leaned down.

"We will find them, Sage."

She swiveled to look at him, her eyes wide and sad. "I just hope we aren't too late."

CHAPTER FOUR

Sage paced her room, her chest tight. She could barely breathe.

She didn't know Simone personally, just knew that she was a scientist aboard the *Helios*. But knowing that she and her daughter were out there, somewhere... The thought broke Sage's heart.

Grace. How could a little girl survive the horror of the Edull?

Sage spun, her hands balling into fists. She wanted to destroy the Edull and make them pay for all the horrors they inflicted.

Breathing heavily, she shoved her hands in her hair, tugging on it until it hurt. She needed to get out.

With a sob, she raced to the door. She wrenched it open and gave a start. Acton was standing outside.

He looked at her, his eyes so cool.

"I... I..." Her throat was too tight to talk.

"Come," he said, turning.

"Where?" she rasped out.

"Out of here."

She wanted so much to touch him. To feel some warmth, some connection. Instead, she followed him down the corridor, her skin feeling like ice.

"I can't stay inside, Acton." The walls were going to swallow her if she didn't get away.

"We'll go out."

He led her out the front doors of the House of Rone, nodding at the two large, silent, cyborg guards. Then, they were in the tunnels beneath the Kor Magna Arena. He moved so fast that she had to hurry to keep up with his long strides

Thankfully, he didn't ask her any questions. He turned a corner and led her into an area where there were bars and restaurants lining the corridors.

Oh. She looked around with interest.

Acton stopped and motioned to one doorway. She walked inside and straightened. It was a restaurant, with large windows that gave her a view of the stone-lined Kor Magna street outside. A few transports zoomed past, along with some carts drawn by alien animals.

Again, there was that fascinating blend of old and modern that she saw all over Carthago.

The restaurant was dotted with tables—some round, some rectangular, some square. She spotted a few familiar faces, and recognized the people as House of Rone staff members.

"Most of the staff that work at the houses frequent this place," Acton said.

A young, male server showed them to a table, casting

wary looks at Acton. Sage wondered if he noticed, but if he did, he showed no reaction.

As she sat down, another server hurried over. The curvy woman glanced at Acton with a half horrified, half curious look on her face.

Suddenly, Sage felt annoyed. Yes, he had metal on him. Yes, he looked cool and remote, but he was a man as well. There was warm flesh under the metal.

"We'll have the mixed taster plate," Acton said. "And some *guarda* juice."

Sage looked at the menu, but couldn't read the alien text. She had a lingual implant that the Thraxians had put in her, so she could understand spoken alien languages, but she couldn't read the writing.

As the server hurried away, Sage scanned the room, taking in all the people. She saw a woman with green skin and silvery hair. *Wow*. Several kids ran past, laughing. There were lots of different species in the place.

Her gaze landed on one being, seated across the room, and her muscles tensed. He had a big, muscled body, with a large set of horns. She tried to swallow, her mouth dry. He looked similar to the Thraxian slavers who'd attacked the *Helios*.

She felt a light brush of a touch on her hand, and jerked her head back. Acton's metal fingers were brushing hers.

"The man is Begatten. They're friendly, a distant relative to the Thraxians."

She nodded. "Right. It's hard to shake old memories sometimes."

"Old memories cannot harm you."

She shot him a sad smile. "It isn't quite that easy to switch your emotions off."

It wasn't long before the server hurried back, setting down the drinks and food. Sage didn't know what everything was, but she trusted Acton's judgment and started to eat.

As she enjoyed the different flavors, she noticed he wasn't touching anything.

"Try this." She offered up a bit of a yummy item that tasted like a soft cheese. "I know you haven't eaten since earlier today."

Dutifully, he took a bite. "It's very...flavorful."

She saw things working in his eyes and hid her smile. Calla had told her that Zaden couldn't handle bold flavors. Sage was suddenly determined to find something that this cyborg liked. She passed him little nibbles of things, watching his face carefully.

"Why are you feeding me?" he asked.

His head was tilted, and she realized that was what he did when he was confused, or trying to work through a problem.

"I want to find something that pleases you."

He stilled, staring at her. She couldn't quite tell why, but she thought he might have been startled.

"Here." It was a piece of a cake that would probably be too sweet for him.

He dipped his head and, as he took the item, his lips brushed her fingers.

Oh. Electricity tingled up her arm. She stilled, and Acton sat back, eating the sweet treat. He got a contemplative look on his face.

Sage hid her smile. He *liked* it. She wanted to do a victory dance. "You like that."

"It is...satisfactory."

She fought a smile, and kept testing the other foods. She found another sweet item, and handed it to him.

"I'm uncertain of the nutritional value of these," he said.

He still ate it. Her cyborg had a sweet tooth.

A tiny feeling of something that felt like contentment filled Sage as she sat there, in the busy restaurant, watching this fascinating cyborg—part man, part machine. He had so many hidden facets, and she really wanted to know him better. She was starting to realize that not many people took the time to get to know Acton.

She also really wanted to touch him. *Bad idea, Sage.* She set her hands in her lap.

All of a sudden, screams broke out on the other side of the restaurant.

Acton's head snapped up.

With a gasp, she turned and watched people leaping to their feet. She froze. "What's happening?"

At that moment, a spider-like robot leaped onto a table. It was the size of a small dog, with six, powerful, jointed legs.

A shiver ran down her spine and her chest tightened. The bot was made of scrap metal—some pieces shiny, others rusted and old. It was a style that was very familiar to her.

Sage leaped to her feet, knocking her chair over. "Acton, those bots are Edull."

He rose, his face sharpening. As they watched, other

bots started to jump on people, and more screams broke out.

"Stay back," Acton ordered.

Then he strode toward the fight.

ACTON SHOVED people out of the way.

"Get to the door," he yelled. "Get out of here!"

He'd already sent a call to the House of Rone for assistance through his comm system.

A spider-like bot leaped at him, its legs spread wide. He grabbed it out of the air, wrestling with it. The construct was strong.

But Acton used his cybernetic arms and his increased strength. The bot's legs crumpled, and then he tore it apart. He threw the pieces onto the ground, watching as they jerked and twitched.

He circled a table and saw a woman on the ground, kicking her legs, her feet hammering against the floor. A spider was attached to her face.

Acton tore it off, revealing blood streaking down her cheeks. She sat up with a sob, and glanced around in shock.

"Go," he ordered, pulling her up.

More shouts and screams echoed off the walls. Nearby, a woman in long skirts was running with her two children. They were being chased by several spider bots.

Acton activated his powers, pumping energy into the air. The bots rose from the ground. He waved his arms, and the bots flew through the air and crashed into the wall with a crunch of metal.

More spider bots poured out of the kitchen.

Acton sucked in a breath. There were too many, but he had to hold them off until help arrived.

He snatched up some plates off the nearest table, throwing them at the spiders.

Several men and women had grabbed makeshift weapons, and were also trying to fight the bots off. One man went down with a scream, several bots scratching at his skin.

Acton jumped, clearing a table and landing with a bend of his knees. He had to wait for the power in his arms to recharge. He kicked one bot off the man and snatched another off.

"Thanks," the man choked out. He staggered to his feet.

Turning, Acton felt energy filling him. He raised his hands and lifted several more bots into the air. They swirled around like a storm and then he slammed them up into the ceiling.

He looked at the dazed, injured people nearby. "Go! Run!"

A heavily bleeding man swiped at his injured chest, but turned, herding people toward the restaurant doors.

Across the room, Acton spotted Sage, and he felt an unfamiliar knock in his chest. She hadn't left. *Drak*. She was in the thick of things, helping an injured family toward the door. A small boy was clutched in her arms, and she reached over, pressing some wadded fabric to an injured woman's face.

Suddenly, a weight hit Acton's back.

He lurched forward, feeling metal claws slashing at his skin. Pain flared, but he blocked it. Reaching over his shoulder, he tried to grip the bot.

Another spider slammed into his chest. Claws sank into his chest, blood flowing down his abdomen.

"Get off him!" Sage's wild yell.

He felt a tug on his back, then the first bot was gone. He grabbed the one on his chest, crunched it into a ball, then tossed it aside.

He quickly swiveled. Sage was holding a wriggling spider in her hands. It was trying desperately to reach her face.

No. He moved in behind her and reached for the bot.

"Let go," he said.

She did, and the bot tumbled onto the floor. He brought his boot down on the robot, with a satisfying crunch. With a snarl, Sage slammed her boot onto the bot. Together, they stomped it into the floor.

"You should have left," he said.

"The correct thing to say is, 'thanks for the help, Sage. I appreciate you getting the robot that was tearing my back up off of me.'"

"Thank you," he said.

"I may not be a gladiator or a cyborg, but I won't let them hurt you."

Something in Acton shifted. She was worried about him? It was a foolish thought, when he was a powerful cyborg who was much stronger than she was. He blinked. No one had ever worried about him before.

"I am very strong and a trained fighter, Sage."

"I don't care. You need to be careful, Acton."

Another high-pitched scream echoed through the room. They both spun to see more frightened customers running from another group of spider bots.

"Help! Help us."

Striding across the room, Acton heaved up a table. He raced at the bots, slamming it down on them and squishing several between the table and the floor.

"Get out of here." People nodded, bolting for the doors in a panicked rush.

He kept fighting back the other spiders. It felt like a never-ending stream.

A child's terrified scream pierced the air.

He turned to see a boy standing on a table. Bots were climbing the table legs, clambering to get to him.

Suddenly, Sage ran at the boy. She was holding a large jug in her hands. She smashed it down on one of the spiders.

"Come on." She helped the boy down. "Run."

She turned to follow the boy when a spider leaped onto her back. Acton saw her fall between two tables, and lost sight of her.

No!

He charged across the room, knocking tables and chairs out of his way. Several bots were racing toward Sage, and he lifted them up with his powers, crushing them together.

He had to get to her. He spotted her on the floor, struggling. Her face was scratched and bleeding.

A spider was attached to her chest, clawing at her.

Acton felt a rush of blind anger—the brightest he'd ever felt—burning through his dampeners.

He roared, grabbed the spider clinging to her, and crushed it in his hands.

Sage was sobbing. He crouched protectively over her, and scanned her body for damage. Her shirt was ripped open. Through the tears, he caught a flash of pale skin, the curve of a small breast, and several bloody scratches.

"Acton." Her voice was drenched in pain.

"Shh." He slid his arms under her and lifted her.

She burrowed against his chest. "I can't breathe."

"It's the panic. Don't worry, I'll get you out. The healers will fix you."

Her hazel eyes met his and she relaxed. Her trust made something inside him go still.

Loud, skittering sounds reached his ears.

He lifted his head and stiffened. A huge group of spider bots skittered out of the kitchen, and surrounded them.

CHAPTER FIVE

S he was bleeding.

Sage swallowed a moan. God, she hurt. And that brought back all kinds of memories she didn't want to remember.

Acton said he'd get her out.

She forced herself to relax a little. He felt strong against her. His chest was warm, and his metal arms were cool.

Dragging her gaze off the wave of bots surrounding them, she looked up at the strong line of his jaw. His face was focused, no fear, no panic.

But when she turned her head, terror pressed down on her like an elephant on her chest. There were so many of the spider bots. Too many. Her throat went tight.

Damn the Edull. She hated them with every fiber of her being. A rush of anger hit her—hot and fierce.

"Put me down," she mumbled. "You can't fight if you're holding me."

Acton hesitated, but when she wiggled in his arms, he

set her on the top of a table. She stood, wavered for a second, then grabbed a dinner knife off the surface. It wasn't very sharp, but it was better than nothing. She felt better having something in her hand.

A spider skittered in, lights blinking on the top of it. Acton lifted his arms and his power activated. She felt the throb of energy in the air.

Several bugs lifted up off the floor, their legs waving madly. One by one, the bugs started to crumple inward, like they were imploding.

The others on the ground were vibrating, waiting to attack.

The first row rushed at them.

"Acton!" she screamed.

He threw his hands out, letting out another blast of power, sending the first wave flying. But she knew he couldn't hold them off much longer.

She lifted her knife, wondering how the hell they were going to survive this. At least, they'd helped all the others get out.

Then the sound of running feet caught her ear, and she glanced over her shoulder. Relief crashed through her.

Magnus strode into the restaurant, electricity crackling down his arm.

Jax was one step behind him, sword in hand, and his tattooed arm glowing. Quinn was next, her lethal staff raised. Mace followed, his large sword glowing red-hot. Toren brought up the rear, the high-tech weapon on his shoulder already activated and swiveling to take aim.

For Sage, time slowed. She watched the cyborgs and Quinn crossing the restaurant, faces grim and focused.

Then time clicked back in with a rush of sound. The cyborgs charged.

The spider bots leaped to attack.

Sage watched the cyborgs *move*. Swords slashed and electricity sizzled. They plowed through the Edull creations, metal tearing and shredding. Acton tossed several of the bots into the air, and Mace swung his sword, his blade cutting through them.

Throat tight, all Sage could do was watch. They were magnificent.

Quinn moved with power and grace, while the others just charged in with raw strength. Acton swiped his arms, and more spiders sailed through the air.

When he lowered his arms, he turned and looked at her.

She smiled.

The remains of the spider bots littered the ground all around the restaurant, and the cyborgs all straightened and lowered their weapons.

But then, her smile died as pain crashed through her. Her legs collapsed.

Oh, no. She was going to tumble off the table.

She didn't fall. Impossibly, Acton moved like a blur and crossed the room in a fraction of a second.

He caught her in his arms. "Sage."

She moaned. Damn, everything was hurting.

He laid her out on the table. "Magnus."

She turned her head, trying to focus on Acton. He sounded...panicked? That didn't make any sense.

"She's losing too much blood," Acton said.

She felt pressure on her chest.

"The bots must have nicked something." Quinn's voice.

The world started to go blurry.

"Acton," Sage whispered.

"I'm here." He wrapped his cool hand around hers. "She needs the healers."

"Avarn is on the way," Magnus said.

Then Acton's face was right in front of hers. She locked onto his icy-blue eyes.

But they didn't really look cool right now.

"Hold on, Sage," he urged.

She tried to nod, but couldn't. She wasn't sure how much time passed, but suddenly, Avarn's face appeared in her vision. The older healer was frowning as he checked her over.

"Acton, keep pressure on her wounds. She needs a regen tank."

Acton lifted her off the table, and there was a blur of movement. Sage drifted in and out of consciousness. Next thing she knew, warm fluid was closing around her body.

"Acton?"

"I'm here. I won't leave you." She felt his cybernetic fingers squeeze hers. "You're in a regen tank."

She recalled the amazing healing tanks from her time helping in Medical. They could heal some of the most terrible injuries she'd seen. The medical tech on Carthago was amazing. Slowly, the pain started to recede, and she squinted and craned her neck to look down. She was covered from her chin to her toes in the blue healing gel.

She also belatedly realized that she was only in her panties, with a small strip of cloth covering her boobs. Not that she had much up top to cover.

Her eyes fluttered closed. Avarn and his healers had explained to her that Magnus spent a fortune on medical equipment to keep his gladiators healthy and fighting fit for the arena. The House of Rone healers were also experts in cyborg technology and cybernetic enhancements.

"You're going to be fine," Acton reassured her.

She forced her eyes open again, turned her head, and saw him sitting beside the tank.

"You got me out," she said.

"I assured you that I would."

"Thank you." She managed to lift a hand over the edge of the glass tank.

He took it, cool metal brushing her warm skin.

"Your wounds are healing."

She smiled. "That's good." She let her eyes drift closed once more. "Keep talking. I like your voice."

He was silent a moment. "You do?"

"Yes."

"What should I talk about?"

"Anything."

Silence reigned for a long moment, punctuated only by the soft noises made by nearby medical equipment, and the gentle movements of the healers throughout the room. When she cracked her eyes open, she saw that she'd confused him.

He cleared his throat. "The Edull clearly planned the attack in the restaurant. The spider bots were definitely Edull constructions."

"Why would they attack that restaurant?"

"The establishment is used by lots of House of Rone workers."

If they couldn't hurt the cyborgs, then they would target the innocent. Her nose wrinkled. "Assholes."

"We will stop them." His voice was firm and sharp as a blade.

"We need to find Simone and Grace." Worry drifted through Sage. Then a wave of tiredness made her eyelids feel like they weighed a ton.

"Rest," Acton said.

She tightened her fingers on his. "Don't leave me."

"I won't."

ACTON SAT by Sage's regen tank for several hours.

Avarn moved closer, his robes rustling quietly. "She's fine. She should wake soon."

Acton nodded. "I'll help her to her room."

The healer eyed him for a long moment, before finally nodding and walking away.

Acton continued to stare at the small woman in the tank. A woman who seemed to spark things in him he didn't want to feel. He hunched his shoulders. In the restaurant, seeing Sage in danger and injured, he'd *felt*.

For the first time in years, he'd had the sensations of

anger, fear... He didn't like it. It was too foreign, too distracting, and dangerous.

His cybernetic eye flickered and a jumble of images hit him—a woman laughing, kids giggling, Metathim soldiers grabbing him, cold fear, his own screams. His pulse spiked and he strengthened his emotional dampeners.

Sage's fingers moved and a moment later, she woke with a gasp. "Acton?"

"I'm here." He reached over the edge of the tank and helped her to sit up.

He looked at her, at the blue gel clinging to her skin. His gaze traced the slope of her shoulder, and then moved up to the slender line of her jaw. She had a graceful neck.

That was an...odd thought for him. Shaking his head, he helped her out of the tank.

She stood in front of him in tiny panties, and a strip of cloth over her breasts. She shivered.

He reached for a drying cloth and started to wipe her down. Her skin color was so pale. As he stroked down her slim arms and legs, he saw that the cloth at her breasts was near-transparent. Her pink nipples clearly showed through.

His body reacted with a throb that made him still.

"Acton?" She tilted her head.

"I'm fine." His cock was heavy and throbbing, an unfamiliar sensation. Confused, he reached out and grabbed one of the robes the healers had left for her. He helped her put her arms into the sleeves, and wrapped it around her.

So, this was physical desire? He glanced at Sage's face, his gaze moving over her cheekbones, her full lips, her copper-colored hair that was damp at the ends. His cock throbbed again.

"Acton?" She frowned, touching his chest lightly. "Are you okay?"

He managed a nod. "You need to rest. I'll show you to your room."

He ushered her out the door of Medical.

"Hey, slow down," she complained.

But he needed to get away from her. He needed to cool his body's unruly response. Still, she was recovering from her injury, so he tried to slow his steps as they walked to her room.

"Are you sure you're okay?" she asked. "You're acting weird."

He didn't answer her, just pushed open the door to her room. Inside, she glanced around and pulled her robe tighter around her body.

"Thanks again, Acton. For everything."

He gave her a tight nod. "I'm happy you're well."

"If you hadn't gotten me out of that restaurant—"

"You're a valued member of the House of Rone now, and we wouldn't want to lose you."

She swallowed, toying with the belt of her robe. "Is that all I am to you? A valued member of the House?"

He felt his spine stiffen, vertebra by vertebra. "You know I don't feel like the others."

She took a step closer to him. "I think you've purposely not let yourself feel." She lifted a hand, moving slowly, like she was waiting for his permission or refusal. "I think you're just very rusty."

He didn't say anything, his gaze locked on her slim fingers. He knew he should turn and leave. Put some distance between them and shore up his dampeners.

She stroked his cheek. His metal one.

Acton sucked in a breath, sensations cascading through his senses.

She was studying him intently. Her fingers moved, stroking his other cheek. The pads of her soft fingers brushed his skin. This time, he shuddered at the onslaught of sensation.

Her lips parted. "Acton." A husky murmur.

He was trying to control his response, but it was over-loading his system. She stepped closer and her body brushed his, her belly grazing against his erection.

She gasped, her gaze dropping. Acton groaned.

"Acton?"

"It is a simple biological response to your state of undress."

She made a humming noise. "I don't buy that."

He gripped her wrist. "I told you, I'm not capable of what the others feel."

She eyed the bulge in his trousers. "This is evidence to the contrary." She leaned in closer, pressing her palms to his chest.

It felt like her hands were burning into his skin. He gripped her wrists, something he thought might be panic sliding along his nerves.

He couldn't handle the overload, this foreign sense of being out of control.

"Sage—"

"You feel, Acton. You've just buried it deep and blocked it out."

"It's too late for me," he said. "Perhaps, if I'd met you earlier, I would have had a chance." He swallowed. "But I've been changed too much."

"I don't believe that," she whispered, color filling her cheeks.

"I don't *want* these emotions free."

Sage flinched. "You don't want to explore them with me?"

"No." He hated this out-of-control, chaotic sensation.

She stepped back, and he felt the loss of her touch instantly. *Drak*, he was so confused.

She gave him a smile, but he didn't detect any humor in it.

"I shouldn't be surprised," she said. "I've never generated enough feeling in anyone to be worth the effort. Not my mother, not my ex."

Acton couldn't process any more emotion. He couldn't read what was buried in her voice, or what was crossing her face. But he knew he didn't like it. "Sage—"

She gripped her robe lapels with one hand and waved the other one. "It's okay, Acton. How I feel is my responsibility not yours. Go now."

His legs refused to move. "I—"

"Just go." This time her voice was sharper. She pressed her hands to her cheeks. "Please. It'll be fine. I'll be fine. And tomorrow, we'll be just as we've always been. Friends."

She gave him one of those smiles she usually gave the

other women. The one he knew she used to hide her true feelings. Then she shoved him out into the corridor. A second later, the door closed in his face.

Acton stayed there for several minutes, staring at the smooth surface of the door. He wasn't sure what had just happened, but he didn't like it, and had no idea what to do about it.

CHAPTER SIX

The next morning, Acton made his way to Magnus's office for a meeting with the other cyborgs.

He'd stopped by to check on Sage first, but he couldn't find her. Her room was empty, and her bed neatly made.

It was for the best. He needed to stay away from her until he could get these strange feelings under control.

As he headed down the corridor, he frowned. He felt unsettled.

When he entered Magnus's office, the imperator nodded from behind his desk. Jax raised a hand. The cyborg was sitting on the edge of Magnus' desk. Mace leaned against the wall, his brawny arms crossed over his chest. He lifted his chin.

"Where's Toren?" Acton asked.

"He's training with Sage," Jax said. "She was up early, and said she wanted to learn some self-defense after yesterday's attack."

With Toren? She was Acton's friend. He would have helped her. A roaring sound filled his ears.

"Acton?" Magnus said.

"Yes." He forced himself to focus on his imperator.

"Do you have your report on the training schedules?"

Acton accessed his records and updated the others on the training schedules for the gladiators and cyborgs. "Xias has requested some new gear for gladiators and their training. I've approved it. The new cyborg recruits are coming along well. Many are above acceptable levels with the various weapons."

"Good. Mace?" Magnus prompted.

The big cyborg reported in on the work of their weapons master, Maxon. The House of Rone had a reputation for making the best weapons on Carthago.

"Maxon is as surly and bad-tempered as always," Mace added. "He's insisting on some cratanium diamond for edging some blades. It's expensive."

"Do it," Magnus said.

"Because you want the cratanium edging or you want to avoid Maxon storming in here and having a tantrum?" Mace asked.

"Both," Magnus replied dryly.

Jax grinned. "All other House business is running smoothly."

Magnus leaned forward, resting his hands on his desk. "And now, onto the subject of the Edull."

Acton straightened, and felt the others sharpen as well.

"I spoke with Zhim and Ryan. The information merchants are following up on some whispers they picked up on. They're following the threads, but don't have anything for us, yet."

Acton knew the two information merchants could finesse any data system. If there was information to find, they'd find it eventually.

"Rillian and Tannon are doing the same, and tapping all the contacts associated with the Dark Nebula."

Rillian was the very wealthy owner of the Dark Nebula Casino. Tannon was his head of security, and they had a large network of informants. They'd all been helping with the search for Bari Batu and the captive humans.

"And Corsair?" Acton asked. The caravan master had been born and raised in the desert. His caravan traversed the dunes, and if anyone knew anything about a lake in the desert, it would be Corsair.

Magnus nodded. "I spoke with him. He doesn't know anything about this lake in the desert. Bari Batu is on the far side of Carthago, well out of Corsair's regular caravan routes. But he knows people who might have information. He's talking with them."

"So, he's heard something," Jax said.

The imperator leaned back in his chair, his cybernetic eye glowing. "It's likely that he's heard old stories, but he won't share anything until he has something solid."

Acton understood. It would be a waste of resources to chase down unsubstantiated rumors. Still, he felt a sense of urgency. A sensation he wasn't accustomed to.

He wanted them to have something so he could reassure Sage that they would find her crew member and her daughter.

Sage. It reminded him of where she was and what she was doing. If she wanted to learn to fight, *he* would teach her. He started for the door.

"Acton?" Magnus said, his voice abrupt.

"I need to go."

Acton charged into the hall. It didn't take him long to reach the training arena. Instantly, he spotted them there across the sand. Sage had a short sword in her hand, and Toren was calling out moves.

Acton frowned. The sword was too heavy for her. He could see that she was having trouble lifting it smoothly.

"Acton?"

He turned his head as Quinn appeared beside him, wearing fighting leathers. She was sweaty, and holding her staff in her hand.

"You okay?" she asked. "You look...more intense than usual. Like something is upsetting you."

He frowned. "I don't f—"

"Feel. Right, except you look like you want to rip Toren's head off."

Acton paused. "Perhaps just one arm."

Quinn snorted. In the arena, Sage missed her swing. When she almost tumbled over, she laughed and Toren smiled.

The muscles in Acton's gut tightened.

"What's going on?" Quinn asked carefully.

"I believe I inadvertently hurt Sage."

The Earth woman tilted her head and leaned on her staff. "Tell me."

"I cared for her after the attack yesterday. I helped her from the regen tank and back to her room."

"Go on."

"My body was..." Maybe it wasn't such a smart idea to talk to Quinn about this.

"I'm not a mind reader, Acton. Tell me."

"I was aroused," he answered tightly.

Quinn's eyes popped open wide. "Oh. *Oh.*"

"Sage expressed some feeling for me. I tried to explain to her that I don't feel enough—"

One of Quinn's eyebrows arched. "If you feel desire, and you're upset that she's upset, your insistence that you don't feel anything smells a lot like bullshit."

Acton had no idea what bullshit was, but Quinn's tone said it wasn't good. "I don't want to feel."

"Now we're getting somewhere." She nodded. "You're starting to feel stronger emotions?"

He fought the urge to hunch his shoulders. "Yes. It is unpleasant and unproductive."

"You're protecting yourself."

He stiffened. "I don't want to hurt Sage—"

"You're out of practice feeling things, and dealing with emotions is hard, Acton. It's messy, chaotic..."

"I dislike mess and chaos."

"I promise you, the payoff can be amazing. But there is always some risk."

He watched Sage swing the sword again.

"If you make her happy, and she makes you happy..." Quinn said. "In the end, it's worth it."

"She said she wasn't surprised that I didn't want her enough. She mentioned her mother and her ex."

Quinn tossed her braid over her shoulder and sniffed. "She hasn't said too much, but I've read between the lines. It sounds like her mother isn't a nice woman. She was pretty indifferent to hearing that Sage was alive."

Acton frowned. "How could someone not want to care for Sage?"

For some reason, Quinn smiled at him. "Sage was dating a man back on Earth when she was on the *Helios*. After he heard the *Helios* was missing, he somehow managed to get over his grief, meet another woman, and now has a child on the way."

Acton processed this information. Sage's mother didn't love her. And her former lover got over loving her very quickly. "I pushed her away and I hurt her."

"Yeah. If you can't give her what she needs, Acton, give her some space and time."

His hands curled into fists.

Quinn reached out and tapped his arm. "But I think if you dig deep, and *let* yourself feel, you might be just what she needs."

He nodded. "Thank you, Quinn."

She eyed him for a second. "Good luck."

He swiveled, striding across the sand to where Toren was leaning far too close to Sage. As he neared, Sage's head snapped up, the sunlight glinting off her copper hair. He saw a mixture of emotions swirl through her eyes before they shuttered.

"Toren, I'll take over Sage's training," he said.

Toren straightened, looking between them. "I think—"

"I wasn't asking," Acton said.

58

His fellow cyborg raised a brow. "Now, Sage asked me—"

"It's fine, Toren." Sage shot the cyborg a bright smile. "Thanks for your help."

Toren looked at both of them for a long moment. "Okay. If you need anything, let me know."

Once Toren had left, Acton turned to face Sage.

SAGE HAD REALLY HOPED to avoid Acton today.

Now, here he was, in all his bare-chested glory. She sucked in a breath. She was covered in a sheen of sweat, muscles wobbly from exertion. Meanwhile, Acton looked icily perfect. His brown hair was neat, his skin its usual, beautiful, gold, and his face a cool mask.

She cleared her throat. "I was training with Toren. I—"

"You'll train with me."

There was something in his voice that she couldn't quite read. "I was fine with Toren."

"You're mine."

Her gaze narrowed. "We're friends." She almost choked on the word. A part of her wanted to throw her stupid sword at him. "I'm House of Rone, like you said. I know everyone here is willing to help me."

Acton stepped closer and the heat of him hit her skin. "*I* will help you."

She huffed out a breath. She'd been so foolish to push things with him yesterday evening. So his body had a biological reaction, that didn't equal feelings. She needed some armor between her and Acton. She needed to keep her own needs locked down. He could hurt her. Badly. That was the last thing she needed.

"Acton—"

"That sword is too heavy for you." He took it from her and strode over to a weapons rack set up by the side of the training arena. She followed him, watching as he set the sword down and then considered the weapons. He picked up two long knives.

"These are better for you." Holding the blades, he held the hilts out to her.

Resigning herself to working with him, she took the weapons. She wished for a second that she was also a damn cyborg and could turn her emotions off.

"Fine." She gripped the hilts. She was relieved that they felt lighter than the sword. But her belly was churning. She really needed some time away from Acton to get her unruly emotions under control.

He led her over to some training dummies and positioned her in front of one.

"Let's do some basic steps and moves first." He pulled a sword off the rack, then demonstrated the moves he wanted her to do.

Sage listened. She followed his footwork, and moved the knives through the air. They felt *much* better than the sword, and were easier for her to lift.

But he worked her hard, and was—unsurprisingly—a perfectionist. Soon, Sage's hair was plastered to her scalp and she was sure her arms were going to fall off.

Finally, he nodded with satisfaction, and they moved closer to the dummy.

"Go," he ordered.

She practiced the moves, stabbing and slashing with the knives. The dummy rocked on its heavy base.

"Good," he said.

His praise filled her with warmth.

"Lift this elbow more." He moved in behind her, his chest pressed to her back.

She closed her eyes for a second. He was so big and warm. When his metal arm brushed her skin, it felt cool, and she liked the contrast.

Air shuddered out of her.

He stilled. "Sage?"

"Go on." Her voice was throaty.

"We'll practice throwing the knives now."

He showed her how to hold and balance the knife. After several practices, the sand was in danger but the dummy wasn't.

"Grr."

"Focus," he said. "You can do this. Possibly. Your aim is not very good."

She wrinkled her nose. "That's a terrible pep talk, Acton."

"I'm just stating facts."

She was going to damn well hit that dummy. She lifted the knife and threw it.

It lodged in the dummy's stomach.

"Yes!" She grinned, feeling pretty damn badass.

Acton crossed his arms. "Again."

Sage threw again and again. She wasn't hitting exactly where she was supposed to, but the dummy had a lot of knife marks on it now.

Finally, her knife whizzed through the air and struck in the central part of the dummy's chest. *Direct hit.*

She jumped up and down. "I did it!"

Flushed from her success, she turned and threw her arms around Acton. He froze.

Oops. "Sorry—" She moved to step back.

"Don't." He wrapped an arm around her and pulled her back to his chest, pinning her in place.

Her cheek pressed against his warm skin, and she heard the heavy beat of his heart. It had a different rhythm to hers, but it was strong and steady.

She breathed in and pulled in the scent of him—musk, metal, leather. Desire, hot and strong, punched through her, leaving her a little dizzy.

Not good.

She wrenched back. "I can't do this."

"What?" he asked with a frown.

"I can't be around you and not touch you." She shoved her hair back. "I can't be just friends. I'm sorry. I want..." She broke off. None of this was his fault. She released a long breath and let her shoulders sag. "It doesn't matter what I want."

"Sage—"

Biting her lip, she shook her head. "This is bad for both of us. You don't want to feel, and I know that feeling can lead to heartbreak."

He frowned. "Hearts can break from feeling?"

"No, it's a metaphor." Her voice dropped. "When you want to be loved, and someone doesn't return the feeling, it hurts. Really hurts."

He stared down at her. "So we should refrain from spending too much time together?"

"Right." Her chest ached. It was the best thing for both of them.

"And we should refrain from touching each other?"

"Yes."

He slid one of his hands into her hair.

She jolted. "Acton, what—?"

He started to massage her scalp with the perfect amount of pressure. "If you want to touch me, then touch me."

Sage blinked, certain she was having a dream while she was awake, or maybe a hallucination. His fingers dug into her scalp and it felt glorious. She moaned.

His hands slid down her neck, finding the knots of tension in her muscles and working on them. She let her head fall forward. His cybernetic fingers were so strong, but he didn't use too much pressure.

"Acton, you're touching me."

"Yes."

She felt so confused, needy, afraid.

"I want to touch you, Sage. I don't want Toren, or anyone else, touching you."

The possessive tone of his voice made her gasp. She tilted her head up to look at him.

He brushed a thumb across her cheekbone.

"You'll need to be patient with me," he urged.

Her lips parted. Was he telling her what she thought he was? "Um, Acton, you're going to have to spell things out for me."

"I want you to teach me to feel, Sage."

She sucked in a breath. "Acton—"

"Acton. Sage." Jax's voice rang across the arena, making them both jolt. They turned.

The cyborg was striding across the sand, his red cloak flaring out behind his powerful body. Sage felt Acton straighten and step away from her. He once again looked like his cool, serious, cyborg self.

"What's happened?" Acton demanded.

"We have news from Corsair," Jax said.

Sage hissed in a breath. She felt the brush of fingers at the center of her back, light as a feather. She glanced at Acton, but saw he was focused on Jax, even though he was touching her.

"Corsair knows someone," Jax said. "An old, desert dweller who remembers ancient stories about a distant desert lake."

"When do we leave?" Acton asked.

"Now."

Sage took a step forward. "I'm coming."

Acton's brow creased. "Sage—"

She shook her head. "Don't even bother trying to talk me out of it."

CHAPTER SEVEN

They moved under the stone archway leading into Varus' stables. Ahead, Acton watched Magnus nod and move to grip the arm of the big, former gladiator. Varus was a burly man, the history of his long time spent in the arena—well before the gladiatorial houses spent fortunes on medical technology—blatantly displayed on his scarred body.

"Welcome," Varus boomed. "It is always a pleasure to do business with the House of Rone."

Acton stayed close to Sage as Varus' stablehands brought out the *tarnids*. He was watching her face the moment she saw the animals.

The big, scaly beasts had six legs, and were built to cover long distances. They intimidated most people, but Sage smiled, reaching out and patting the neck of the fierce animal.

"Many people are afraid of *tarnids*," he said.

"I told you that I like unique things." She patted the *tarnid*'s dark-green scales. "You're beautiful, aren't you?"

Acton gripped her waist and lifted her up onto the beast. She made a squeaking sound, but then settled. He swung up behind her and she made another small noise.

He stilled. "Are you okay?"

She nodded, glancing back over her shoulder to smile.

Acton pulled in a breath, and under the heavy scent of animal, he detected a musky, spicy scent.

She was aroused. His body vibrated. Instead of blocking the emotions, he let them flow, accepting them. He tightened his arm around her, then he leaned forward and pulled in the scent of her hair.

"Are you sniffing my hair?" she said.

"Is that not acceptable?"

A smile flirted on her lips. "I don't mind. Sniff away."

Ahead, Magnus, Jax, and Toren mounted their *tarnids*. Mace scowled for a second before climbing on his. He didn't enjoy riding.

A thought occurred to Acton. "Will you be okay being back in the desert?"

"I'll be fine." Sage's voice was filled with solid determination.

Magnus led the way, and soon the *tarnids'* hooves clicked on the stone road as they made their way out of the city. It wasn't long before the desert sands opened up ahead of them.

Sage pulled the light-weight scarf around her neck up over her head. She'd changed into typical loose-fitting, pale-colored desert clothes.

"Are you sure you're all right?" he asked again.

She nodded. "The desert's gorgeous in a stark,

dangerous way. Besides, I was locked in the Edull's cells and labs most of the time. I never saw much of the desert itself."

Acton tightened his grip on her, his palm pressed against her belly. It was intriguingly soft, with a hint of tone beneath it. She was so pretty, and he couldn't stop looking at the way the sunlight glinted off her hair. It lit up the strands in different shades of orange and gold.

He stared at her and felt a muscle work in his jaw. She was breaking down barriers inside him. He knew he wasn't equipped to deal with how his body responded to her.

But he had an enhanced intellect and he was a fast learner. He would deal with it. He flexed his fingers on her and heard her suck in a breath.

He turned her reaction over in his head. "You like that?"

Not looking at him, she nodded.

He stroked his hand up her belly again, caressing her hipbone. She shifted restlessly on the *tarnid*.

"Acton—"

"Yes?"

"I want to touch you," she whispered.

He looked ahead. They were at the rear of the group, the other cyborgs ahead of them. But he was well aware that they all had enhanced senses.

"We can't, not here. Besides, I'm afraid my control won't be good enough."

"Later?" She looked up at him. "When we're alone?"

He nodded.

They continued to ride, and Sage appeared to enjoy

watching the changing desert terrain. He grabbed the water bladder hanging off the side of the *tarnid* and made her drink. He had also pocketed some *panella* before they'd left. When he handed her the sweets, she beamed at him.

"They'll help keep your energy up," he said.

Her smile widened and Acton felt like he'd won a fight.

"Tell me about Tiarla," she said. "I'm guessing there are no deserts there?"

His homeworld was such a distant memory that it took a moment to try and remember. "No. It was verdant farmland, and gentle, rolling hills."

"And you were taken from your family?"

His muscles stiffened. "Yes. The Metathim Military came every few years. They were based on a neighboring planet. They took some of the strongest teenagers to join their military. A few who were most suitable, were sent to the cyborg program."

Sage gasped. "What about your parents?"

"They couldn't fight them. The Metathim would have razed the farms and villages to the ground."

"They didn't even try to fight for you?" she asked.

"I think most people who had strong sons and daughters figured it was inevitable." He paused. "The Metathim try to minimize the memories of all the people they take. They didn't have the tech to erase memories completely, but they could dull them. My memories are so faded that I don't even remember my parents' faces."

Sage shifted, looking upset. Was she sad for him?

"It was a long time ago, Sage."

"But being taken from your family, your choices stolen, that leaves scars."

He realized that her situation wasn't much different to the one he'd lived through.

"Scars help us grow and learn," he said.

Suddenly, she jerked, and he detected movement to the side of their *tarnid*. A *mull*. The small, desert animal bounded off into the sand, burrowing deep to escape them.

"Oh, that looked so cute," she said.

"It's called a *mull*."

"It's so fluffy."

"It is a very good hunter. It doesn't generally attack people, but it can be savage."

Sage grimaced. "Of course, it can. Everything out here seems dangerous."

They continued on, and Acton spotted something ahead in the distance. "There's the caravan."

Sage peered ahead and huffed out a breath. "Your eyesight is much better than mine."

Moments later, she saw the wagons and smiled. "Oh, wow."

The caravan was made up of a variety of transports, and several tethered *tarnids* milled around.

Acton took in the vehicles, tents, and animals. Sage probably didn't notice, but he saw how the transports formed a safe perimeter, with the tents in the center. Corsair protected his people and his caravan.

As soon as the cyborgs pulled up, young children in desert clothes raced over to take the leads of their *tarnids*.

A young girl with a huge, shaggy canine sitting by her

feet waved at them. Sage waved back. The canine stared at them balefully.

"Magnus," a deep voice drawled.

The newcomer strode forward, a slight swagger in his walk, and a streamlined bird of prey perched on his shoulder. He had a muscled body clothed in typical desert gear, with a dark leather belt, and a well-worn leather bandolier across his chest. His brown hair was shaggy and streaked with gold, no doubt due to life under the desert suns. His eyes were golden brown.

"Well, he sure packs a punch," Sage murmured.

Acton paused. Did she find Corsair attractive? Corsair looked and acted nothing like Acton. He was a man who smiled easily, and clearly felt a gamut of emotion. As Corsair spoke with Magnus, his hunting bird lifted off into the sky.

Frowning, Acton slid off the *tarnid* and lifted Sage down.

A large man and slender woman approached behind Corsair. The man was Bren Hahn, an accomplished hunter. The woman with the dark hair was his mate, Mersi Kassar. They were Corsair's right hands and his best friends. They helped with the day-to-day running of the caravan.

Then, the sharp crack of canvas being slapped open. Another woman strode out of a tent. She walked with economic movements, in a way that said she knew how to carry herself. Her dark hair was pulled back in a braid. She was a taller, sharper version of Ever Haynes.

The woman pinned Magnus with a hard stare. "How are my sister and niece?"

"Excellent, Neve," the imperator replied.

Neve sniffed. "Make sure they stay that way, cyborg."

Corsair slid an arm around Neve's shoulders and grinned. "Be nice to your brother-in-law."

Neve's nose wrinkled. Then her green gaze landed on Sage. "You must be Sage."

Sage nodded. "Sage McAlister. Nice to meet you."

"Neve Haynes, Ever's sister."

The women shook hands and Acton stepped forward, staying close.

Neve's eyes flicked up to him. "You have a cyborg bodyguard?"

Sage's lips curled. "I guess I do."

"Come." Corsair waved an arm.

The caravan master led them deeper into the caravan. They passed crowds of people—some clearly members of the caravan, and others passengers. Corsair stopped at an area that had a bright-red shade cloth strung above it, flapping in the breeze. Beneath it, there was an area with well-used rugs.

"Would anyone like something to drink?" Mersi asked.

"Sage would, Mersi," Acton answered.

Sage rolled her eyes. "How about you ask me first?"

"But you need to stay hydrated."

She rolled her eyes again. "Thank you, I'd love a drink."

Mersi's lips twitched, her purple eyes glowing. "And you, cyborg?"

"I do not require any sustenance right now."

"He always talk like that?" Mersi asked.

Sage smiled. "Yes. You get used to it."

Soon, they were all seated around on the rugs. Magnus leaned forward, one knee raised and his arm resting on it. "Who is this desert dweller you said has information for us?"

"An old man," Corsair said. "He's older than anyone I know. He's forgotten more about the desert than I've ever learned."

"Where is he?" Acton asked.

"Mia Gedi. A tiny oasis not far from here."

"Then let's go," Sage urged. "Simone and her daughter are out there, somewhere, and we *have* to find them."

"Things move slower in the desert, Sage," the caravan master said. "We'll leave shortly, once your *tarnids* are rested and watered. We will do everything to find your friends." He ran a hand down Neve's dark braid. "I promise you."

Acton sensed Sage's upset. He reached out and brushed his fingers against hers on the rug. Sage jerked, then looked down at his fingers. Her gaze moved to his face.

Then her fingers closed on his.

Acton hadn't felt anything before that felt so right.

SAGE ENJOYED RIDING on the *tarnid*.

After their short stop at the Corsair Caravan, they were now headed deeper into the desert. Not that she was looking at the stark scenery. She wasn't even focused on the feeling of the powerful animal beneath her.

Instead, all she could think about was being surrounded by Acton.

Last night, she'd barely slept, consumed by hurt and embarrassment.

Now...

She blew out a breath. A part of her was terrified. That this thing between her and Acton wouldn't work. That he'd change his mind about exploring emotions. That he'd decide she wasn't worth the risk. That he'd break her heart.

Closing her eyes, she forced some air into her lungs. Despite her fear, she couldn't seem to stay away from him.

She now knew that he'd been torn from his family. He'd had cyborg enhancements forced on him. The Metathim Military had stolen his memories, his emotions, and buried them deep.

And Sage was going to drag him, and what he felt, back into the light.

She'd teach him to live again.

"I can see trees," Acton murmured.

She strained to see. She couldn't see any trees, but she just didn't have Acton's super-duper eyesight. Then, light glinted off what had to be a pool of water.

Corsair pulled ahead of the group. He wasn't riding a *tarnid*, but a different desert animal with two long legs that reminded her of an ostrich. It had a long neck and beige scales, and was called a *morloch*.

It wasn't much longer before the oasis came into

view. It was tiny and almost picturesque, with the pool of dark water ringed by trees. The trees had long trunks and deep-purple foliage that spread out overhead like a lattice.

Right beside the water was a small, domed hut made from beige stone.

As their group pulled in and slid off the *tarnids*, a dog-like creature bounded out from behind the hut. It barked at them with deep, resonant *woofs*.

"Nice, big canine," Jax muttered.

A man came shuffling out of the hut.

Sage blinked, then stared at him, taking in his wrinkled, tanned skin. His silver hair was so long it brushed the sand at his feet.

Suddenly, she sensed all the cyborgs stiffening around her. They were all staring at the pool of water.

Something stirred within its depths. Water rippled, implying a big *something*, and a shiver went down Sage's spine.

Whatever lived in the water was enormous.

Acton's arms tightened on her.

"Garrolf, enough." The man's wavering voice was still filled with a core of strength, like the endless desert. The canine went quiet.

"Derma, my other pet—" the man jerked his head toward the pond "—she won't hurt you."

The ripples in the water subsided, but the tension in the cyborgs didn't.

"Tolpan." Corsair strode forward to greet the man.

The old man gripped Corsair's hand vigorously. "Corsair, how is that fierce woman of yours?"

74

"Still fierce. Just yesterday, I woke up with a knife pinned through my sleeve."

Tolpan let out a rasping laugh. "I'm sure you deserved it." Then his cloudy gaze turned and zeroed in on the House of Rone cyborgs. "Cyborgs."

Magnus inclined his head. "From the House of Rone."

"I hear your house does good things, Rone. And you make good weapons."

Magnus drew a small dagger off his belt and handed it over. "A gift."

Tolpan's eyes widened. "Made by Maxon?"

"Of course."

Wrinkled fingers stroked the blade. "That man is a genius."

"Please don't tell him that," Jax said. "He's a grumpy, temperamental, and egotistical one."

Tolpan made a harrumphing sound that could have been a laugh. Sage didn't see him move, but suddenly the knife was gone, hidden in the folds of the old man's desert robes. Then his milky gaze settled on Sage.

"You're not a cyborg."

"No, just a woman."

"Hmm. From the same world as Corsair's feisty Neve."

Sage nodded. "Earth."

"The Thraxians took you too?"

Her belly tightened, and she sensed Acton shift closer, the warmth of him at her back. But she lifted her chin, facing the ugly memories head-on.

"Yes. They sold me to the Edull."

Tolpan made an angry noise and spat on the sand. "Arrogant, know-it-all scavengers."

"They're keeping other humans captive at Bari Batu," Sage said quietly. "Including a child. We have to find them and free them."

Tolpan stared at her for a beat, then swiveled with a rustle of robes. "Come." He disappeared into his hut.

Corsair stooped through the small opening and inside the hut.

"Mace and Toren, I want you on patrol," Magnus said.

The cyborgs nodded. Then the imperator went inside, followed by Jax. Sage ducked through the doorway, with Acton right behind her. Inside, it felt as though the temperature dropped several degrees.

She scanned the dim interior. A skylight in the ceiling let light into the hut. It wasn't fancy, but it was comfortable, with cool, stone walls, and worn rugs and cushions on the floor.

The canine came in and went straight to a huge cushion. It circled around, getting comfy, then settled down with a doggy groan. But it was watching them.

Tolpan sat on a cushion, moving agilely for a man his age. Not that Sage knew his exact age, but he had to be very old.

"My father told stories of when the Edull first appeared on Carthago. They stripped metal like hungry *nakar* flies, and were always full of grandiose plans. And happy to run over anyone who got in their way. Like insects, they multiplied."

Sage settled on a cushion and Acton sat beside her. She tilted sideways into his body.

"That sounds like the Edull," she said through a tight throat.

She felt fingers brush the back of her hair. Acton was touching her again, trying to offer comfort.

Tolpan watched her, an inscrutable look on his face. "The Edull started with an outpost, but as they grew, they built their scrap city."

"Have you visited it?" Magnus asked.

"No. Just heard stories."

"They kept me at an outpost," Sage said. "Locked in a lab."

The man muttered a word her implant couldn't translate, but she was pretty sure it was a curse.

Then he rose in a surprisingly smooth move. He puttered around, lifting a battered kettle from some sort of hotplate.

"You don't know where Bari Batu is, do you?" Sage asked.

"If I did know once, I've since forgotten." Regret crossed Tolpan's lined face. "I'm very old." He poured two steaming drinks, dunking in some strange leaves.

He handed one cup to Sage, and took the other for himself. Then he sat and sipped the tea.

Sage cupped her drink and tried it. She barely registered the strong taste, instead, focusing on fighting back the frustration searing along her veins.

She wanted to know where Bari Batu was. She wanted to find Simone and Grace.

"You'd risk your life for these other humans?" Tolpan peered at her over the rim of his cup.

"Yes." Sage leaned forward. "I can't enjoy my new life, knowing that I'm safe, when Simone and Grace are captives." Sage's voice hitched. "I know what the Edull can do."

"Hmm. And the cyborgs, they risk themselves as well?"

"Yes, the House of Rone has done so much to rescue me, and some other women, as well. Quinn, Jayna, Calla."

Tolpan eyed Magnus and Acton. "But they're machines."

Sage set her cup down with a hard *thump*. "They are *men*. Flesh with metal, but they have hearts. They are honorable to the core. The Edull aren't cyborgs, but they are unfeeling assholes. Flesh alone doesn't make you better than anyone."

The old desert man smiled, and suddenly Sage felt as though she'd passed some sort of test.

"You are fierce, like Corsair's Neve."

"I'm just me," Sage said. "I'm not a fighter, but I will do what I can to find my crew members."

"My aunt, who long turned back to sand, visited the Great Lake of the Edull."

Sage sucked in a breath and felt Acton tense.

"My memories are old and faded, but I believe it was near the Stone Sea of Suffering."

Sage grimaced. *Sea of Suffering?*

"I haven't heard of that," Magnus said, frowning.

"I don't have fancy coordinates," Tolpan said "But I

can tell you that it's past the Red Dunes of Tauri. And it's well hidden."

"Hidden?" Magnus asked. "How?"

"I don't remember. I'm old."

Looking at Tolpan, Sage saw tiredness wash over him. He seemed to shrink in on himself, the lines on his face deepening and the light in his eyes fading.

"Past the Red Dunes, and then look for the daggers."

The daggers? Sage wondered what the hell that could be.

"I'm tired," Tolpan said. "Please, go now. I need to rest."

With a nod, Magnus rose and headed for the door.

Sage stood, then hesitated. "Thank you."

Suddenly, Tolpan reached out and grabbed her wrist. His gnarled grip was surprisingly strong.

Acton surged closer, his big body tensing in battle readiness.

"Be careful, Sage from Earth," Tolpan murmured. "The desert tests us all to our limits." His gaze flicked to Acton. "Don't falter when it matters most. He needs your heart."

Sage stared in awe at the otherworldly look in the old man's eyes. Acton slid an arm around her.

"Delve deep, cyborg," Tolpan said. "She needs you to be her shield, her protector."

Then the old man sank back on the cushions, waving them off.

CHAPTER EIGHT

The desert suns felt far hotter now.

On the way back to the caravan, Sage found herself drowsing and fighting the urge to nod off. She trusted Acton to keep her upright on the *tarnid*.

As her thoughts drifted, she remembered Tolpan's words. *They had a lead to the lake.*

She bit her lip. *Hold on, Simone. Hold on, Grace.*

Sage *had* to believe that mother and daughter were both still alive. She had to hold on to the belief that they would get them out of whatever hellhole the Edull had stuck them in.

Behind her, Acton tensed. She lifted her head and saw the other cyborgs staring intensely at the horizon.

"What is it?" she asked.

"It looks like a sandstorm," Acton said.

Great. Just what they needed, to get blasted by sand.

It wasn't long before Sage could also make out the cloud of brown-beige sand hovering in the air ahead.

Then Corsair bit out a curse. "That's not natural. Something's causing it, and it's coming this way."

Magnus held up a hand and the cyborgs pulled their *tarnids* to a stop. The imperator slid off his beast, staring ahead.

"It's robots," he said.

Sage sucked in a breath, her belly tensing. *The Edull.* It had to be.

"Sage."

She looked at Acton. He'd dismounted and reached up to help her down. Once her boots hit sand, he pressed two knives into her hands. Her fingers closed on the hilts, and she realized they were the ones she'd trained with.

"You stay back with the *tarnids*," he ordered.

She swallowed. A deep, angry part of her wanted to fight, to let loose the rage that simmered inside her belly. These were the aliens who'd kept her captive, hurt her.

But she wasn't a fighter, and she didn't want to get in the way of Acton and the other cyborgs.

Ahead, Magnus and Jax were standing shoulder to shoulder. Their powerful bodies were battle-ready and alert.

Mace strode forward, his boots kicking up sand, and drew his sword. Toren came up on the other side, a weapon rising up out of the metal plates on his shoulder. It swiveled to take aim.

Corsair joined them, his jaw hard as he stared at the incoming sandstorm. She watched him reach over his shoulder and pull a sword. As soon as it was free of its sheath, it lit up, glowing electric blue.

They'd fight. To protect her, and to take the Edull down.

She turned and gripped Acton's harness. "Be careful. I don't want you hurt."

He stared at her for a long moment, then gave her a solemn nod.

Something told her that he wasn't used to someone being worried about him.

"Not a scratch, Acton."

"I am difficult to kill."

Then he strode toward the others. Her gaze dropped, taking in his perfectly formed ass. A hysterical laugh bubbled in her throat. Of all the times for her to be ogling his butt.

She focused on trying to calm her nerves.

As the storm approached, the *tarnids* became agitated, stomping at the sand. Sage moved among them, patting their necks to try and calm them.

It wasn't long before the robots crested the rise of a dune, coming into view.

Ten, fifteen, twenty. She lost count, a stone settling in her stomach. She sucked in a breath. They looked like...*centaurs*.

In typical Edull construction, they were pieced together with bits of scrap metal. They had four huge, powerful legs, strong bodies, and a humanoid torso at the front.

Goddamn Edull.

Then the centaurs charged, their hooves pounding on the sand. One of the *tarnids* panicked, and Sage tried to grasp the reins. The powerful beast broke free, running off into the desert.

"No!" she cried.

She watched the *tarnid* sprint away. All of a sudden, one of the centaurs broke away from the pack. It arrowed toward the runaway *tarnid*, picking up speed. As it neared the *tarnid*, it reared up, bringing its front hooves down on the animal.

A sharp, terrified whinny pierced the air.

Oh, shit. Horrified, Sage watched the *tarnid* collapse and hit the sand.

Magnus' arm flared, electricity crackling along it. "Leave and we won't destroy you." His voice boomed, somehow amplified beyond his normal volume.

With a clank of metal, the centaurs formed into a line ahead of the cyborgs.

For one hopeful second, Sage thought the bots might back down.

Then they charged.

The centaur bots raced toward the cyborgs. Her hand tightened on her knives, her heart hammering in her chest.

Magnus and Jax leaped high, crashing into the lead centaurs. Sparks of electricity flew through the air.

The cyborgs' powerful bodies moved, spinning and dodging. Jax rammed into a centaur and Magnus followed, thrusting a fist into the side of a bot. It collapsed in a shower of metal parts.

Toren fired his laser bolts. The blasts ricocheted between several centaurs, blowing holes through the metal.

With a roar, Mace raced in, his sword raised above his head. It glowed hot and red, and when he swung it at a charging centaur, the blade sliced through the metal like it was butter. As he spun to face the next bot, Sage watched metal flow over Mace's skin, turning him into a living shield.

Corsair appeared, running fast. The caravan master looked small as a centaur reared above him. He slid in feet-first, slipping under the centaur, and slicing its belly open with his sword.

Then Sage's gaze locked onto Acton. He lifted his arms and a centaur bot rose into the air. It twisted and jerked, then Acton tossed it so it crashed into another.

The fight was hard and fast. Several of the Edull's bots had fallen to the sand. She dragged in a breath. The cyborgs were winning. She smiled darkly. *Take that, Edull scum.*

Then, a centaur broke through the line and charged past the cyborgs.

It was coming right at her.

Shit. Her body locked. The *tarnids* let out angry snorts and huffs. *Shit, shit, shit.* She lifted her knives.

The bot raced toward her, its eyes glowing bright green, the ground vibrating beneath her feet.

Then suddenly, a big body slammed into the centaur from the side, making it stumble.

Acton.

Sage's pulse went into overdrive. She watched as Acton slammed the bot to the ground. It wildly kicked its legs, and one huge hoof hit Acton right in the gut.

He flew back and hit the ground.

The centaur rose, hooves pawing the sand.

No! Sage ran at them, lifting her knives.

The centaur took a step toward Acton, but Sage leaped up, ramming her knife into the centaur's metal face.

Suddenly, the bot's arms swung out and hit her. *Ow.* She crashed back to the sand, rolling over and over.

Her ribs throbbed. She tasted sand in her mouth.

"Do not touch her."

Acton was up. He launched himself at the bot, and leaped onto the centaur's back. With his cybernetic arms, he reached into the metal casing and ripped it open. The centaur bucked and reared.

Acton held on with his knees. Sage saw his face and gasped. He was in a terrible, focused rage. He kept tearing at the bot, ripping chunks of metal off. Then he gripped the centaur's head and, with a massive heave, he tore the bot's head off.

As the robot's big body collapsed, Acton leaped back onto the sand. "Sage."

"I'm okay." She rose, shaking sand out of her hair.

He leaned down and yanked her knife out of the bot's decapitated head. He held it out to her and she took it.

"Are you all right?" she asked.

A swift nod. "Minor injuries."

They both turned to assess the situation. The other centaurs were all down and scrap metal littered the sand. The Rone cyborgs were gathered together, kicking at the remains.

One bot moved sluggishly. Its body was still intact, but its legs were mangled.

"Definitely Edull construction," Magnus said.

The centaur's head swiveled, its eyes glowing eerily. "There are more of us."

A chill went down Sage's spine.

"You won't reach the caravan in time," the bot finished.

Corsair cursed, running for his *morloch*.

Acton raised his hand and the centaur's head crumpled.

"Let's move," Magnus said. "Fast."

ACTON HELD on to Sage tightly, one arm wrapped around her waist. They raced across the sands, pushing the *tarnids* as fast as they could go.

They were closing in on the caravan. Corsair was far ahead of them, his beast able to run much faster than the *tarnids*. Toren was riding with Mace, so they were bringing up the rear.

A *boom* echoed through the air and Sage jerked. "What was that?"

"A defensive turret." Acton heard the fighting now. More cannon *booms* followed.

Sage's hands clenched on his wrists. "What's happening?"

He used his enhanced vision to zoom in. "The caravan has moved into a protective formation and have activated their defenses." He saw a slim figure out on the sand fighting a centaur. *Neve.*

Near the woman was a big, broad-shouldered form holding a wicked crossbow. Bren.

Corsair reached them first, leaping off his *morloch*. He whirled his electroblade and joined the fight.

The House of Rone cyborgs slid off their *tarnids* and charged in. Magnus was in the lead, ready to fight.

"Stay back," Acton warned.

Sage nodded. "Go."

A part of him didn't want to leave her, but she gave him a shove and he jogged toward his fellow cyborgs.

A flash of movement. A centaur was racing in from the sidelines, aiming directly at Neve. Acton opened his mouth to yell a warning, but the woman spun, then leaped into the air. She landed on the bot's back and started stabbing it.

He shook his head. These Earth women were extremely unpredictable.

The centaur bucked wildly and Neve lost her grip. She flew through the air.

"Neve!" Corsair yelled.

Acton rushed forward and flung his arms up. He caught her with his kinetic power and lowered her to the ground.

"Thanks." She looked at him, her face almost as unreadable as a cyborg's.

He set her down gently, and together, they eyed the incoming centaurs.

A considering look crossed her face. "Can you throw me, cyborg?"

He nodded.

She lifted her weapon and then Acton moved his

fingers. Neve rose off the ground. He moved his arms and she sailed through the air. As she whizzed past a bot, she slashed it with her sword.

Acton moved her again, and she cut into another centaur, and another.

His power almost depleted, he moved her back toward him. As her boots touched the sand, she laughed.

"That was awesome."

"Happy to help."

"You aren't too bad, cyborg."

Screams broke out.

Neve swiveled. "Oh, fuck."

Two centaurs had broken into the caravan. Corsair was already running, the other cyborgs just behind him.

Acton raced forward. Mersi was firing a weapon, standing in front of a group of travelers and children.

The centaurs were converging on her.

"Mersi!" Bren bellowed.

Seeing his mate threatened, the big man put on a burst of speed. Acton watched as something black and oil-like spilled out over Bren's skin, completely covering him.

Drak. Acton stared as Bren morphed, his hands tipped with claws. The man let out a deafening roar and ripped into the centaurs.

Bren was Tainted.

Acton had heard of Taint—dark microbes that lived in hidden pools in the desert. If ingested, it transformed the infected. He hadn't known that any of the Tainted could have this kind of control. The myths said they were ravaging, wild creatures that needed to be hunted down.

He watched as Bren punched his fists through a centaur, destroying it.

Then a woman screamed. "One of them took my son! Help!"

Acton turned. A centaur was pounding away from the caravan, a terrified child clutched in its arms.

Then a *tarnid* came into view, racing after the bot.

Sage. Acton felt a hot spike of fear. Sage was hunched over the back of the galloping *tarnid*, giving chase.

He sprinted after her.

"Acton!" Magnus yelled.

He wasn't stopping. He kept his gaze on Sage. He pushed for every bit of speed his cyborg system possessed, the world blurring around him.

Sage neared the centaur and he saw her rise up out of the saddle.

No. *No.*

She jumped off her *tarnid*, landing on the back of the centaur. She almost slid off, but clamped on with her arms and legs. She managed to sit up and started smacking at the bot's head, stabbing it with her knife.

The bot released its hold on the boy. Sage dived off and grabbed him, the pair of them rolling through the sand, barely missing the bot's thundering hooves.

The centaur slid to a halt, turning to face them.

Acton's heart thumped hard in his chest. He pushed for more speed, but he'd already calculated the odds that the centaur would reach the pair before him.

He was too far away.

And he wasn't close enough to use his cybernetic power.

But... Acton threw up his arms.

His power swirled around him, and he focused hard, pulling sand into a funnel. He moved his arms and the mini-sandstorm moved toward the centaur.

The bot took a few steps back, but then it was engulfed.

The centaur spun and its hooves left the ground. It struggled desperately to break free, but the sand continued to swirl around it.

Acton ran toward them, shutting off his power. The bot slammed to the ground, but Acton lunged. He landed a hard kick to the bot's side, crumpling the metal. He followed through with a punch with his cybernetic arm, then another.

The centaur staggered, but then it kicked out with its rear legs, slamming into Acton's gut. He flew back several feet.

Sage had pulled the boy away and was crouched, covering him with her body. Protecting him.

As Acton would protect her. He wouldn't fail her.

He attacked the bot again. It reared up, trying to kick him. He dodged to the side.

Then Jax arrived, breathing heavily. His tattoo was alive with energy.

"Pin it," Jax ordered.

Acton dredged up what power he had left. Bracing, he threw his arms out, his body alive with energy. The centaur's legs became glued to the ground, and it fought viciously to get free. Jax strode close, then rammed his arm into the guts of the centaur. Electricity skated over the metal.

The centaur shuddered, then collapsed into a pile of metal parts.

Acton lowered his arms. Sage lifted her head, and he saw a frightened boy watching them with huge, blue eyes.

"Rix," Corsair yelled.

With a sob, the boy broke free of Sage's arms. He ran to the caravan master and Corsair lifted the boy off his feet, hugging him hard.

Acton knelt beside Sage and she leaped into his arms.

He wrapped his arms around her and pulled her close. He sensed the others watching them, but ignored them all.

"You were supposed to stay back." He was shocked to find his voice was unsteady.

"Sorry." She pressed her face against his neck. "I couldn't let them take that boy."

Of course, she couldn't. Acton dusted the sand from her hair and held on.

CHAPTER NINE

"There you go." Sage pressed a bandage over an older man's eye.

"Thank you, young lady." He gave her a nod.

Sage turned, gathering up some of the first aid items that Mersi had given her to treat the caravan's injured. Luckily, the worst of it seemed to be cuts and bruises.

Next, she smiled at a young girl. Shyly, the girl sat down and held out her leg. A nasty scratch ran down the girl's shin.

"Ow, that must sting. Let's make it better." Sage started cleaning the girl's wound.

All around, the Corsair Caravan was righting itself. The cyborgs were pitching in with the cleanup, while Sage and the caravan's healers helped the wounded. She had to admit, these desert people were tough and resilient. They got on with things and didn't dwell.

"All done," Sage said. "You were very brave."

The girl offered her another smile and scampered off.

Sage let her hands fall to her thighs. This felt good. Helping and using her skills again. For the first time in a long time, she was enjoying it, and feeling a little more like herself.

She looked over and spotted Acton helping to right an overturned transport. He and Mace heaved, lifting the transport back onto its wheels.

"Thanks for rescuing Rix," a female voice said.

Sage turned and squinted into the sun. Neve stood over her, casting a shadow.

Rising, Sage dusted off her trousers. "I wasn't going to let the Edull snatch him."

Acton turned, his strong, lean body in profile. Of course, her gaze snagged on the flex of his ass.

"So, you have a thing for one of the cyborgs, huh?"

Sage jerked. "Um." She tucked a strand of hair behind her ear.

"He seems..." Neve's gaze arrowed on Acton. "More cyborg than the others."

"There is still a man under the enhancements."

Neve nodded. "Well, good luck. You deserve to find your happiness, Sage."

Sage's throat tightened. But could Acton give her that happiness?

Suddenly, Magnus straightened, touching his temple. Then he spun to Jax. She saw the men talking urgently and watched as Jax stiffened.

"House of Rone," Magnus called out. "Mount up. Fast."

With a nod at Neve, Sage hurried over. "What's going on?"

The line of Magnus' jaw was hard. "I just got word that the House of Rone is under attack."

She gasped, looking around the caravan. "This was all just a diversion."

Acton urged her over to the *tarnid* and lifted her onto the beast.

By the time he pulled himself up behind her, Magnus and Jax were already heading off into the desert. Mace and Toren mounted their animals—one loaned to them by Corsair to replace the animal they'd lost. The cyborgs urged the *tarnids* into a fast gallop.

Their group raced toward Kor Magna. With every beat of the *tarnid*'s hooves, worry pounded through Sage. Were Quinn, Jayna, and Calla okay? What about Ever and Asha? God, there were so many kids at the House of Rone.

"Do not worry," Acton said.

"That's impossible. I can't just switch it off."

"We have many fighters in residence—gladiators and cyborgs. And our allies are close by."

Like the House of Galen. Swallowing, Sage nodded, but she was still worried. "All these attacks, they keep delaying us from searching for Bari Batu." Leaving Simone and Grace enslaved.

"We will not let the Edull beat us. We *will* find your crewmate and her child."

Sage sighed. "Thank you, Acton."

"It's my job."

"No, there's a loyal, honorable guy inside you."

He blinked, looking surprised. She smiled briefly. She liked surprising him.

Finally, the city appeared on the horizon. As they reached the outskirts, Magnus didn't slow down. They thundered through the streets of the city, heading toward the arena. Pedestrians and vehicles scattered at the cyborg onrush.

Stone walls rose above them, the flags slapping in the breeze at the top. Several plumes of smoke were rising in the distance. The sight was like a fist to her belly.

"Oh, God."

When they reached the arena, they leaped off the *tarnids*. Magnus was already charging into the tunnels. The cyborgs sprinted toward the House of Rone, and Sage struggled to keep up.

They rounded a corner and were greeted by the sound of fighting.

Humanoid robots were battling in the tunnel with several gladiators and cyborgs. Sage scanned the mêlée, attempting to take it all in.

Quinn swung her staff, slamming it into one bot. Zaden was beside her, using his powerful telekinetic abilities. He lifted several bots into the air and mangled them together, then he thrust them into the wall.

Other gladiators from the House of Rone were swinging swords and axes, each of them covered in sweat, grime, and blood.

A flash of red fabric caught her eye. Raiden Tiago, Champion of the Kor Magna Arena from the House of Galen, charged into several bots, his swords flashing. Imperator Galen was fighting beside him—hard and unrelenting—his black cloak flapping behind him.

"Sage," Acton barked.

"I'll stay back. Go." She saw he was vibrating with the need to join the fight.

She pressed a hand to the stone wall and watched as Acton and the other cyborgs raced into the battle.

THE STENCH of smoke was sharp in Acton's nostrils. Ahead, he could see that a section of wall beside the House of Rone doors had been knocked down by some sort of explosion.

A robot came at him, its heavy, piston arms pumping. He kicked it, and then used his cybernetic powers to slam it into the ground. He stomped on it until its lights blinked out.

He swiveled, just as something fell from above him.

Slender bots were clinging to the stone ceiling. One crashed into him, and he wrestled it to the floor.

Acton grunted, straining against it. *Drak*, the thing was strong.

They rolled across the ground, slamming into some debris.

Toren stepped into view, his weapon aimed downward. With one blast of laser, the bot's head exploded.

Acton sat up. He heard a roar, and watched Magnus tear a bot apart.

The imperator glowed with fury.

Nearby, Xias charged. His teeth were bared as he spun, ramming his sword into another bot, sparks flying. "Take that, you sand-sucking crudspawn."

Several bots were backing up now, realizing that they were about to be overwhelmed. A few started to retreat.

"Xias," Magnus said.

"We won't let them get away." The gladiator broke into a run, several gladiators falling in with him. They sprinted after the escaping bots.

"Quinn." Jax embraced his woman, yanking her off her feet. She wrapped her long legs around Jax's waist.

Mace shouldered forward. "Jayna?"

"She's fine." Quinn tossed her sweat-soaked braid back over her shoulder. "Locked in Medical with Ever, Asha, and the rest of the house workers and children."

Acton scanned the ruins of the bots, cursing the Edull. Smoke hung in the corridor, the stench sharp in his senses. Then he spotted something and crouched. Frowning, he lifted a piece of the bot in his hand and rose. "Magnus?"

The imperator scowled.

"It has organic parts," Acton said.

They all stared at the sinew and flesh that made up part of the bot's internal workings.

Magnus' face turned even more grim. "That's why they've stepped up taking more slaves, and increased their experimentation in their labs."

"They're creating bots with organic parts," Jax breathed. "We saw one large bot in Gaarl's lair with organic parts. I thought it was just his own experimentation."

Acton had been a man once, fully flesh and bone. Now, he had enhancements, but this...it was an abomination. This piecemeal creation, with organic parts stolen from unwilling slaves, was beyond evil.

He heard quiet footsteps and looked up to see Sage walking toward him. He released a breath. She looked fine, relief in her eyes.

Something moved in the smoke behind her.

He tensed. "Sage!"

She froze. A bot reared up behind her. It had been lying on the ground, but clearly hadn't been destroyed.

Sage spun, but the bot was on her in a flash. It lifted her off her feet and threw her over its shoulder. She hammered her fists against its metal back.

Acton and the others were already moving, but the bot spun and sprinted down the tunnel. It moved blindingly fast.

Acton's boots slapped on the stone floor as he chased the bot. He wouldn't let the *drakking* thing take Sage.

He watched her body bouncing around on the bot's shoulder as they barreled through the tunnels.

They turned a corner, and he heard screaming. The bot slammed through a group of people, knocking them to the ground.

Acton leaped over the downed people. He got close to the bot, his gaze meeting Sage's wide eyes. He dived, tackling the bot around the knees.

They all fell with a crash.

Sage broke free with a cry and rolled away across the stone floor.

Acton landed on the bot, trying to keep it pinned. Suddenly, its head swiveled around, and its mouth opened. A strange, red fluid sprayed out, landing on Acton's arms.

The fluid burned, eating into the metal.

He punched the bot, then reached for his powers.

Nothing.

He tried again. Still nothing.

Whatever the bot had sprayed on him had deactivated or damaged his cybernetics.

Rising, he kicked the bot.

It shoved up and swung an arm at him. Acton realized his own arms were useless. He couldn't move them.

The bot kicked at him and Acton stumbled back. It charged again and Acton fell. He rolled backward, and sensing weakness, the bot rushed at him.

"Leave him alone." Sage ran at the bot. She darted between Acton and the bot.

"Sage, no!"

She rammed her knife into a patch of skin in the center of the bot's chest.

The construct stopped and shuddered.

Acton pushed himself to his feet and rushed forward. He kicked the bot and it crashed to the ground, slamming into the wall. Acton kicked again, and again.

He heard running footsteps, and knew that the rest of the House of Rone had arrived.

"We've got it." Jax went down on one knee, checking that the bot was disabled. Then he gripped the bot's neck, charged his arm, and electrocuted it.

The bot fell to pieces.

Sage turned. "Acton."

His vision was blurring, and pain was tearing through

his body. He collapsed, sitting down hard on the ground. The pain was agonizing.

"Acton!" She knelt in front of him, stroking his cheeks. "God, your arms."

He glanced down. The fluid was eating through his metallic skin, exposing the wiring beneath.

"It hurts."

She cupped his cheek, her face fierce. "We'll get you to Avarn. Hold on, baby."

Baby? His last coherent thought was to wonder why she was calling him baby.

CHAPTER TEN

As Acton slumped against Sage, they almost toppled over. Jeez, he weighed a ton.

She locked her muscles and held him sitting upright. He was hurt, and her chest throbbed with worry for him.

Mace crouched down beside them and slid a muscled arm around him. "I've got him."

"Thanks, Mace." She patted Acton's side. "You're going to be fine."

As the big cyborg lifted Acton, Sage scrambled to her feet. Ahead, Magnus barked out orders.

"Jax, take a team and check every part of the House of Rone. Make sure no bots are left."

"On it." Jax jogged inside, his cloak flaring behind him.

"Toren, clear the destroyed bots and organize repairs to the wall."

The blond cyborg nodded.

Sage followed Mace through the doors. "He's hurt really badly." Her voice cracked.

Mace jerked his head. "Avarn will fix him up."

When they made it to Medical, Mace thumped on the door. "Avarn, this is Mace. Everything's safe. Open up."

The doors opened and people poured out. House workers raced into the corridor. Everything became a blur for Sage. The healers burst into action, but all she could see were the lines of pain around Acton's mouth.

"Over here." Avarn pointed to a bunk, his face creased with concern.

Mace laid Acton down.

Then suddenly, Jayna was there, leaping into Mace's arms.

"Sage?" Ever appeared, Asha on her hip. "Are you all right?"

She glanced up and nodded. "Magnus is coordinating the cleanup. He'll want to see you." She turned back to Acton and saw his eyes had opened. She stroked his cheek. "Hey, how are you doing?"

He blinked slowly. "Tired."

"I know. I'm here. Rest."

His eyes closed.

She made herself watch as Avarn started repairing Acton's arms. He took several slender tools, digging into the holes eaten in Acton's arms. He made several unhappy noises as he worked.

"Need to repair some wiring," Avarn muttered.

The healer lifted a scanner running it over Acton's body.

"You're good with him," Avarn said.

"He's...helped me a lot. I like being with him."

"Apart from the other cyborgs, no one's ever taken the time to look beneath his strength and his cyborg parts. And that includes Acton. He believes he's incapable of being just a man."

"I won't let him keep hiding." She smiled, brushing Acton's hair off his forehead. "I'm stubborn like that."

Avarn lifted a tool, working on a part of Acton's arm. "You Earth women have stubborn persistence by the cargo hold."

"Yep. When you're smaller, you have to fight harder and smarter."

Next, the healer pressed small metal patches over the holes dotting Acton's arms. The small patches appeared to melt, covering the holes like they'd never been there.

"He's lucky." The older man patted her on the shoulder. Then he touched a pressure injector to Acton's neck. "You can go, cyborg. But take it easy for a day until you recharge."

Acton's eyes opened and he sat up, looking groggy and exhausted. "Thank you, Avarn."

As he swung his legs off the side of the bed, Sage moved closer.

"Lean on me."

His brows drew together. "I'll crush you."

"I'm tougher than that."

They hobbled through the hubbub of Medical and out the door. She helped him down the corridor, hating that he seemed so weak and was moving so slowly. This wasn't the Acton she knew. Finally, she got him into his quarters.

The room was shadowed and impossibly neat and tidy. No messy clothes or knickknacks.

"Thank you, Sage—"

"I'm not leaving."

His brows drew together.

"I'm going to take care of you." She urged him onto the bed, and he dropped down heavily. "You protect everyone, Acton, but now it's my turn."

"I don't need you to take care of me."

His words made her suck in her breath, pain a tight ball in her chest.

He watched her carefully, his brow creasing. "I hurt you?"

Suck it up, Sage. He's still learning to deal with emotion. "Yes, but you didn't mean to. I know you don't need me to take care of you, but I'm still going to do it."

She reached up and unbuckled his harness, sliding it off. Then she moved into the bathroom. She found a bowl and filled it with water. Then found a cloth.

When she returned, he'd removed his boots and was leaning back against the pillows. She sat on the edge of the bed and started washing his face. His gaze flicked up to hers.

Sage's belly flooded with warmth at the emotion in her cyborg's eyes.

She washed his chest, cleaning away the blood and grime. She ran the cloth along the joint between skin and metal.

"You have a beautiful body, Acton. All this golden skin, lean muscles, smooth metal."

She rinsed the cloth and then stroked lower, washing his hard stomach. He sucked in a breath.

"You need to get these trousers off." She flicked open the button on his leathers.

He stiffened.

"It's fine, Acton. I'm not going to hurt you."

After a beat, he lifted his hips, and she slid his trousers down his body. They were tight on him, and she huffed a little until she finally managed to pull them over his feet.

That left him wearing a pair of snug, black boxers. With a hard swallow, she dipped the cloth in the water again, then ran the damp fabric up his strong thighs.

As she moved upward, she noticed the hard bulge in his boxers. She licked her lips. *Oh.*

"I need to shower," he said abruptly, moving to sit up.

"Will you be—?"

"I'll be fine." He pushed to his feet, and moved unsteadily toward the bathroom. He closed the door.

Sage bit her lip. She knew he'd reached the limit of his strength and endurance. Worried, she hovered near the doorway, in case he needed help.

But after a short shower, he was back, brown hair damp and with only a drying cloth wrapped around his waist. He didn't meet her gaze.

As he moved back onto the bed, Sage went into the bathroom and discarded the bowl and cloth. She took a few moments to wash her face and freshen up a little.

When she returned to the bedroom, he was lying on the bed with his eyes closed. She reached out and touched his face. He had ridiculously long eyelashes.

She slid one hand over his shoulder and those eyelashes fluttered.

"Do you like that?" she asked.

"I like you touching me." He pulled her down onto the bed beside him. "Too much."

"I like touching you, so there's no problem in that."

"I...worry about my control."

She smiled. "I don't want your control. Can I...touch you some more, Acton?"

There was a beat of silence, then he nodded. "Please."

EVEN IN THE DIM ROOM, Acton saw that Sage's face was flushed. She reached out and stroked his chest.

So much sensation. All of it good. He was tired, his systems running on empty, his barriers low. Not that it mattered, the sensations Sage generated broke through his dampeners anyway, like they weren't even there.

Her fingers drifted lower, taking the time to explore. She traced her nails over his abdomen.

"So strong," she murmured.

She played with the muscle at his hip, seemingly entranced. He sucked in a breath, a cascade of heat rushing over him.

"That's good?" she asked.

He nodded. "More."

Her hands were on his thighs now, kneading the muscles. Then she gripped the drying cloth and pulled it away.

His cock rose up, hard and engorged.

"Acton—" Her voice vibrated with desire.

"Touch me, Sage. Please."

Her fingers dug into his thighs. "Are you sure?"

"Yes." He reached down and grabbed her hand, pulling it to his throbbing cock.

Her fingers tightened around him and she stroked. He jerked. His groan echoed in the room.

"You're all man, Acton."

Right then, he felt it. He was pure sensation, with unfamiliar emotions storming through him.

"Sage." As she stroked him, his hips pumped upward. "I've never...never shared this with anyone before."

Her breath hitched. "I kind of like that." She leaned closer and her warm breath puffed across his chest. "I like that I'm the only one who's touched you here."

He slid a hand into her pretty hair.

"What do you want, Acton?" she murmured.

He didn't know. For the first time in his life, he couldn't think and he felt too much. And it was all centered on the woman watching him with hot, sensual intensity.

"You like me touching you?" she asked.

He nodded, his throat dry.

Her fingers worked his cock, and then she lowered her head.

He didn't realize what she was planning to do until she sucked the head of his cock into her mouth.

"*Drak.*" His hand twisted in her hair. "Sage, what are you—?"

"I want to taste you." She was panting, need in her eyes.

"Why?"

She smiled. "Because I want to pleasure you. Because doing this to you pleasures me."

He saw the way her body was shifting restlessly on the bed. He scented her musky arousal. "You're aroused?"

She nodded. "Tell me what you want, Acton."

So few people had ever asked him that. He only had one answer. Right now, all he wanted was Sage.

"You. Protected, safe, happy. Your pleasure."

Her pretty lips tipped upward. "*This* will give me pleasure."

He licked his lips. "Take what you want."

She shook her head. "Tell me, Acton."

His chest was tight, but he managed to draw a breath. "Suck my cock. Please."

Her grip tightened and her head lowered, copper hair spilling across his skin. She sucked him deep.

A shout broke from him, his chest heaving. He grabbed the covers, watching her kneeling there between his legs, her pretty mouth stretched around his cock.

She bobbed up and down on his erection, her face suffused with pleasure. One of her hands gripped his thigh, her fingers digging into a small metal implant there. Her fingers moved, caressing it.

He groaned again and then she slid up, licking the head of his cock like a sweet treat.

"Sage—" His control was gone, burned away. He bumped his hips up again and she moaned, taking him deep. He felt a wave of something growing inside him, something big that was about to break. "Sage."

"Come, Acton. I'm here." She sucked again.

His release ripped through him and he growled. He pumped into Sage's warm mouth. She sucked hard, swallowing everything as he came.

When Acton sank back on the bed, he couldn't think. He was used to lightning-quick clarity, but as he looked down at Sage, he couldn't form a single word. She smiled up at him, licking him and then nuzzling his stomach with her cheek. His body shuddered.

She looked...pleased. Happy.

She slid her body up his. "I've thought of doing that with you for a while. Driving you wild."

What had he ever done to deserve this woman? To deserve to bask in all her bright light?

"Sage." It was all he could manage.

She nestled against his chest. "You're a gorgeous man, Acton." Then she kissed him, soft and gentle. "Now you need to rest."

He frowned at her "What about your pleasure?"

"Later." She pressed into him. "When you've rested."

He pulled her close and she nuzzled his neck. "What are you doing?"

"Snuggling." She rubbed her cheek on his skin. "I love a good cuddle. I'm going to sleep with you."

Acton had never slept with anyone before. He'd never wanted to.

But this—her warm weight close—it felt good.

Besides, it meant she'd be close to him, where he

could protect her all night long. Something inside him loosened.

"Sleep," she ordered.

Acton pulled her closer, and with her scent teasing his senses, he shut down and slept.

CHAPTER ELEVEN

S age drifted out of sleep, sighing. She was pressed against a hard, warm body. A cool, firm arm was wrapped around her waist.

Acton.

She turned her head and watched him sleep. His face was the most relaxed she'd seen it, his hair mussed. He looked much more man than the enhanced cyborg warrior he was.

Then his eyes flicked open.

"Hey," she murmured.

"Good morning." He sounded instantly alert.

She sat up, and her shirt fell down one shoulder. "How do you feel?"

His brow creased like he was uncertain how to answer.

She pressed a hand to his chest. "Don't overthink it."

"I feel healed. I have no pain." He tilted his head, his gaze on her bare shoulder. "And I feel...good waking beside you."

Warmth wormed through her, and when he lifted a hand and stroked her shoulder, she shivered. There was a look of wonder on his face.

"You like that?" he asked.

"I like it anytime you touch me."

He pulled in a deep breath. She reached up and pushed the shirt farther down, until it pooled at her waist.

His gaze went to her bare breasts, light igniting in his eyes. "You are so pretty."

"Thank you." Those heartfelt words arrowed right to her heart.

"Can I touch you, Sage?"

"Yes. Yes, please."

He lifted his hands, gently cupping her breasts. Sage swallowed a moan.

"Your skin is cool." Her voice was husky. "It feels so good because I'm too warm. Do you like touching me?"

"Yes. You're so soft." His fingers shifted, rubbing both her nipples.

Now she moaned. Sensations rippled through her, straight to her core.

He stilled, his gaze on her face. Then he caressed her breasts, working her nipples into hard points. "You're very sensitive here."

"God, that feels so good, Acton."

His organic cheek was streaked with color. His gaze was glued to her breasts.

She closed her eyes and whimpered. He pushed her back onto the bed, and then shoved her shirt down her hips, followed by her loose-fitting trousers.

She saw his nostrils flare, his hands stroking up her legs. His metal fingers brushed her inner thigh.

"Yes, touch me," she murmured. "Higher."

One hand slid higher, skimming across her panties. He touched her again and her hips jerked.

He stilled, a finger brushing against the damp fabric. "You're so wet."

"You make me like that."

"A biological response so that your body is prepared for—" His eyes flared.

She bit down on her lip. "Yes."

"I wish I had organic flesh on my fingers—"

She shook her head. "I don't. You're perfect just as you are."

Another wild flash in his eyes. His fingers twisted in her panties, and then he tore them off her.

Sage gasped. Then his cool fingers slid through her swollen folds.

"Oh, *oh*." She panted, her hips lifting.

Acton paused.

"Don't you stop! Please don't stop."

His fingers dragged through where she was slick and warm. His thumb bumped against her clit.

"Yes!" Her back arched.

"You like that." His voice was a growl, deeper and more edgy than she'd ever heard it.

"Yes."

He leaned over her, his cybernetic eye glowing neon. "Tell me, Sage. Tell me how to pleasure you."

Need was tearing through her, the pleasure so acute

it was close to pain. His fingers kept stroking her and she could barely breathe. His eyes were on her like a laser.

"That small nub, it's my clitoris. A bundle of nerves that gives intense pleasure when stimulated. But other things feel good too."

"I want to make you feel good."

"Slide..." she had to clear her throat "...slide a finger inside me."

Instantly, he obeyed, nudging her thighs wider and pushing one finger inside her.

She cried out. "That's so *good*."

Acton leaned down, sucking one of her nipples into his mouth. She pushed up against him—the warmth of his mouth sucking on her breast, the cool, thick finger plunging inside her... It was all too much, and at the same time, not enough.

"Acton..."

"Tell me what you need."

"I want you to taste me."

He lifted his head, his lips glistening from sucking on her. He stared at her face.

"Between my legs," she urged him.

He moved fast, sliding down her body and pushing her thighs farther apart. His big palms slid under her bottom, his breath warm on her skin.

She threaded her fingers in his hair and watched as he leaned in, his face sliding along her thigh.

"Acton!" So much sensation coursing through her.

He stared at her, where she was hot and swollen, until she wanted to squirm. Then he buried his face between her thighs.

Sage screamed his name. He licked at her, dragging his tongue over sensitized flesh. He opened his mouth wider, and he sucked and licked. When he groaned, the sound vibrated through her.

Then he found her clit.

She tightened her hold on his hair. "Oh, God. Acton."

His tongue swirled, and he made a hungry sound that she felt right in her lower belly. His mouth closed over her clit and he sucked.

Her orgasm hit like fire ripping through her. She screamed, arching into his mouth.

He kept working her, eating her like he couldn't get enough of the taste of her.

And her cyborg held her tight as she trembled through her release.

NEED—DARK and intense—rocketed through Acton. He watched Sage come apart, pleasure all over her pretty face.

He'd done that. He'd given her what she needed and made her feel like this.

Throbbing, needy sensation washed through him, and his breathing turned harsh. His organic skin felt over-sensitive. Even the receptors in his metal skin were firing. Everything was overwhelming.

The air around him filled with energy, and he realized he'd lost his grip on his cybernetic power.

He glanced up and several items—a dagger, a leather

harness, their discarded clothes, a chair—floated in the air, swirling around the bed.

Sage—with heavy lids and a flushed face—gasped. Her eyes widened, and she pulled the sheet to her chest.

"Acton?"

"I... It's too much."

"It's okay." She cupped his cheeks. "Just focus on me."

He locked his gaze with hers.

She smiled. "We'll just have to go a little slower and practice some more." She stroked his skin, sliding her fingers down his neck and stroking his metal implant. "You are so handsome."

He listened to the silk of her voice, letting it slide over him. "No one's ever said that before."

"You never let anyone close enough." Her thumb rubbed against his jaw.

Around them, all the floating items dropped back down. The chair tipped over with a *thud*.

"There." She leaned forward and brushed her nose against his.

Slowly, Acton regained some control. The roar in his blood dimmed a little.

Then there was a loud knock on the door.

"Acton." Mace's deep voice.

"I'm here." Acton answered, grabbing the drying cloth off the ground, and wrapping it around his waist.

Suddenly, the door flung open, and Sage squeaked.

Belatedly, Acton realized that she was naked under the sheet. He quickly flipped the fabric over her head.

Mace entered and stopped abruptly. *"Drak,"* the big cyborg muttered.

"Hi, Mace," Sage called out.

The cyborg made a strangled sound and Acton straightened.

"Do you need something, Mace?"

The cyborg's lips twitched. "This is *not* a situation I ever imagined you in."

Acton tilted his head. Sage's bare leg wasn't covered by the sheet, and he reached out and stroked it. "Me, neither."

Mace grinned. "How the mighty have fallen."

Acton raised a brow, feeling...unusual. He felt a strange need to smile. "I'm just following your path. One you've already crashed down. At least I'm not tearing up training dummies in the arena and denying my feelings."

Mace looked at the items littered across the floor and the overturned chair. "At least I didn't lose control of my powers and toss things around."

Sage's head popped up. "Can we hurry this along?"

The sheet slipped a little, exposing the slope of her shoulder and the top of her breast.

Frowning, Acton shifted, blocking Mace's view. When he looked back, Mace was smiling.

"We have a planning meeting to find the lake," Mace said.

Sage sat up, keeping the sheet clutched to her chest. "I'm coming."

Acton pushed her back down. "We'll be there."

Mace stomped out the door. "Put some clothes on."

As soon as the door closed, Sage bounced up and off

the bed. She leaned over and smacked a kiss against Acton's lips. "Let's get going."

His fingers flexed on her and she smiled. He towed her back in and kissed her again, slow and gentle.

She made a humming noise. He followed her movements, mimicking her as her tongue delved into his mouth.

"You're getting pretty good at that," she murmured.

"I am a big believer in practice to hone one's skills."

"I bet," she murmured. "We'll get back to this later."

He nodded, staring at her mouth.

She smiled now, bright as the sun. "Head in the game, cyborg." Her face turned serious. "We need to find that lake. We need to find Grace and Simone."

He nodded and quickly set about pulling on some fresh clothes. They went past her room, and she changed into a pretty green top and trousers.

When they arrived at Magnus's office, all of his screens were filled with images. The first picture Acton saw displayed showed huge, red sand dunes.

Sage walked ahead of him, stepping closer to the screens on the wall. "Did you find the lake?"

"Not yet." It was Quinn who answered. The woman was eyeing Sage, then she looked to Acton, a slow smile spreading across her face.

"These are the Red Dunes of Tauri," Magnus said.

"Tolpan said to go past them and look for the daggers," Sage said.

Quinn's nose wrinkled. "We have no idea what the daggers are, yet."

Acton watched Sage's shoulders sag. Following

instinct, he slid an arm around her. He'd seen the other men do it so many times with their mates, and when she leaned into him, he knew he'd done the right thing.

He felt plenty of interested gazes on them.

"We'll find it," he told her.

In front of them, Magnus nodded. "We're running searches. We have limited images of the area, so it'll take time."

Sage tensed and Acton squeezed her. She blew out a breath and nodded. "I know I need to be patient, but it's damn hard."

"The House of Rone is fighting the House of Loden in the arena today," Quinn said. "We're all going."

Sage frowned. "We can't have fun while Simone and Grace are out there."

"You can and you will," Quinn said. "We all need to recharge. We'll do them no good if we run ourselves into the ground." Quinn's gaze flicked to Acton and back. "You're entitled to a life, Sage."

Sage looked torn.

Quinn linked her arm through Sage's. "Come on. We'll go and find Ever, Jayna, and Calla." She looked at the cyborgs. "We'll meet you at the arena."

Acton watched Quinn tug Sage out the door. She managed to shoot him a smile before she was gone.

"Soooo," Jax drawled.

Magnus leaned forward, a serious look on his face as he pinned Acton with his stare. "What's happening between you and Sage?"

Mace grunted. "Found her naked in his bed this morning."

"What?" Toren looked shocked, his eyes gleaming.

"We are..." Acton usually found words direct and easy. "It's..."

Jax laughed. "I *like* this. Mr. I-don't-understand-why-these-Earth-women-are-tying-you-up-in-knots is tongue-tied over a pretty, copper-haired Earth woman."

Acton blew out a breath. "She awakens things in me. I can't stay away from her. I don't want to stay away from her."

"Head over heels." A smile touched Magnus' lips. "That's what Ever would say."

"I'm not certain I can give her what she needs," Acton said quietly.

"She'll show you, Acton," the imperator said. "Protect her, listen to her. The rest will fall into place."

Protect her. That he could do.

CHAPTER TWELVE

———————————

The thunder of the crowd rocked through Sage, rattling her bones.

She grinned. The huge arena was filled with wild energy and a sense of eager anticipation.

The stone seat beneath her was hard, and she shifted to keep her butt from falling asleep. Down in the center of the arena, the gladiators were already out on the sand, waving to the crowd and doing test swings of their weapons.

The Kor Magna Arena was packed, and the sand-covered floor looked completely different to the last time she'd been here. Instead of flat sand, there was a rocky landscape, and even some trees, dotted here and there.

"It's holographic," Ever yelled over the noise of the cheers.

She was bouncing Asha on her knee. The tiny girl wore a small set of futuristic-looking earmuffs to protect her hearing.

On the other side of Sage, Calla smiled. The alien

woman was practically glowing, her dark hair tumbling around her face that was lined with the pretty, gold patterns of her species. Since she'd moved into Zaden's rooms, the woman was clearly happy.

She'd come a long way from when she'd been locked up with Sage.

The timbre of the crowd changed. Down below, the competitors were performing wild leaps and jumps, deep-green cloaks accenting their fighting leathers. The House of Loden.

Then Xias, the House of Rone champion, threw his arms wide and let out a wild roar. The crowd roared back, and the other Rone gladiators waved their weapons.

Moments later, the gladiators lined up, and after a horn sounded, the fight began.

Sage watched Xias bound over the rocks, light on his feet for such a big man. Weapons clashed, sometimes sending sparks flying, and the crowd booed and cheered.

"This is just what we needed," Ever said.

Sage nodded. Despite her worry for Simone and Grace, being here, all her senses engaged in watching the fight, helped clear her head. She had to admit that she felt better than she had in a *long* time.

And Acton. *Oh, boy.* She felt her cheeks flush.

Ever eyed her, her lips twitching. "You look pleased with yourself."

Sage just smiled in reply.

Like she'd summoned him, Acton arrived with the rest of the cyborgs. A big group of broad-shouldered badasses. She saw several members of the crowd turn to watch them.

Jax moved over to Quinn, nudging her with his hip to sit beside her. Like he was being towed into a black hole, Mace hurried straight to Jayna. He scooped the woman up, sat, and nestled her down in his lap. The tall, silver-eyed Zaden sat beside Calla and wound his fingers through hers.

Acton's gaze moved to Sage, and she tilted her head and smiled. He moved over, standing behind her. She felt a faint brush of fingers on the back of her neck, the sensation sending goose bumps over her body.

Magnus sat on the other side of Ever and took Asha from his mate. The baby grinned at him and smacked his face. The imperator smiled, before turning his gaze to the fight.

A female cyborg brought up the rear of the group. Sage had seen Seren before, and she'd never, ever seen a woman who looked so dark and dangerous. The female cyborg's black hair was pulled up in a high ponytail, and her sharp face was dominated by purple-blue eyes and black markings that winged out from her eyes and ran down her cheeks. She also had small, horn-like metal implants on her forehead.

"Hi, Seren," Ever said.

The female cyborg inclined her head in greeting, and then turned to stand at the railing.

Sage got the sense that the woman wished she could be in the fight. But Seren had several enhancements—a mix of silver and black metal—which meant she was excluded from the arena. Sage wondered idly what abilities her enhancements gave her.

Suddenly, the crowd booed. Sage arched her neck

and looked down to see Xias cornered by a huge, fur-covered beast and a Loden gladiator.

She leaned forward, her belly tightening.

"He's fine."

Acton's breath puffed on the back of her neck. She shivered.

"He'll use the beast to appear beaten, then go in for the kill," Acton said.

Sure enough, Xias engaged the beast. It roared and slashed out with sharp claws. It looked like a tough fight, with the gladiator swinging his sword hard and fast. Claws caught his chest, leaving bloody grooves.

The crowd gasped.

Finally, Xias slashed his sword across the beast's belly and it collapsed on the ground.

The Rone gladiator rose, his upper body marred with scratches, and blood dripping down his dark skin.

His rival from the House of Loden sensed weakness and rushed in for the kill. He swung a wicked, metal staff with spikes on the end of it.

The staff smacked into Xias' gut and he staggered. The crowd gasped again.

The Loden gladiator smiled and strode forward.

Then Xias spun, grinned, and charged. He surprised the unprepared gladiator, and skewered the man through the shoulder with his sword.

The Loden gladiator fell to his knees, and Xias moved his sword, pressing it to the man's throat. The crowd erupted in screams. He pumped a fist at them.

"He's too cocky," Seren said, disapproval in her voice.

"It's part of the fight," Jax countered. "Fighting in the arena is part fight, part showmanship."

Seren sniffed, clearly unimpressed.

Xias turned slowly, yelling at the crowd.

His fans yelled back, and nearby, a group of women hung over the railing. They were shouting some rather interesting propositions to Xias and throwing—Sage squinted—their underwear at the gladiator.

Sage blushed and laughed.

Xias grinned, pointing at the women. They broke into giggles, and his smile widened against his sweat-sheened skin.

Then the gladiator turned to look at Magnus. The imperator nodded and Xias bowed his head.

When the champion raised his head, his gaze clashed with Seren's.

Sage's gaze went to the female cyborg and she saw the woman scowl. Then Xias' smile took on a sharp edge. He tipped a mocking salute at the cyborg.

Sage was so focused on the interaction between the two that it took her a second to realize that the screams of the crowd behind her had changed.

They'd turned from jubilant to terrified.

She swiveled her head. Around her, the cyborgs leaped to their feet. Sage rose, but she couldn't see around the broad shoulders.

"What's happening?" she asked.

"*Drak.*" Jax drew his sword.

"Ever," Magnus said. "Get Asha out of here."

The crowd surged, panicking. People were trying to

rush to the exits, but they were trampling others in the process.

"It's too dangerous for the women to move," Jax said.

A muscle ticked in the imperator's jaw. "Form up."

Sage, Jayna, Calla, and Ever found themselves surrounded by a wall of muscle and metal. Sage watched the remaining cyborgs draw their weapons.

Acton was right in front of her, and Sage touched his back, leaning around him to see.

Robots were bounding through the stands.

She sucked in a breath. People were running and screaming.

Those shithead Edull.

These bots were lizard-like, with heavy tails covered in spikes. One jumped onto a row of stone seats and swung its tail. It hit a man, and he flew backward with a scream.

Suddenly, Seren charged past. The female cyborg took two steps and she *disappeared.*

Sage blinked, her pulse jumping. Then the woman reappeared right near the lizard bot, with what looked like black smoke shimmering behind her.

Teleportation. *Holy cow.*

Seren drew two huge combat forks from the sheaths on her thighs. She rammed one into the lizard and sparks erupted.

Quinn, Jax, and Mace ran into the fight, weapons swinging. From nearby, laser fire whined, and Sage knew it was Toren.

She watched a glowing blue bolt arrow toward one bot. Just before it reached the robot, it split into several small, glowing pieces. The lasers slammed into the bot, tearing fist-sized holes through the metal.

Three bots rose into the air. Zaden strode forward, his arm raised. He moved his arm and the bots flew out over the central arena and crashed into a wall.

Magnus and Acton stayed back, forming a shield in front of Ever, Sage, and the others.

Then Sage heard more noises and turned. *Oh, God.* There were robots down on the arena floor. Xias, the House of Rone gladiators, and the House of Loden gladiators were fighting them.

But some bots broke away, bounding toward the wall right below her. When they reached the wall, the lizards started climbing up the stone.

"Acton!" she yelled. "Magnus!"

The cyborgs swiveled and both cursed.

Acton leaned over and threw his arms out. She felt the beat of his energy as he pushed the lizards off the wall.

But as soon as they hit the sand, they righted themselves and started climbing again.

There were too many.

"I need a weapon," Sage said.

Acton turned his head and hesitated. Then he pulled a knife from his belt. She grabbed it, her fingers squeezing the hilt.

Magnus pushed closer to Ever, who was clutching a panicked Asha to her chest. He nudged them away from the railing.

"Here they come," Acton said.

The first wave of lizard bots climbed over the railing. Sage jabbed out with her knife, hitting one.

Its tail swung and she dodged the spikes. When it swung again, she ducked underneath, and rammed her knife into it. The lizard fell backward, crashing down to the arena floor.

Magnus reached past her, touching several lizards, and electrocuting them with his cybernetic arm.

Acton had his sword in hand, swinging at the robots each time they got near the railing.

Sage turned and saw more bots were bounding down the stands. Damn, they were surrounded. The bots seemed to be converging right on the House of Rone group.

The cyborgs were all focused, fighting hard.

Then Sage saw one sneaky lizard dart low, aiming for Ever.

Oh, no, you don't. Sage jumped in front of Ever and Asha let out a cry. Sage kicked the lizard. It flipped onto its back and she dropped on it, stabbing it with her knife.

Its mouth opened and it struggled to get free.

Dammit, it was strong. She gritted her teeth and stabbed again.

Then Acton was there. He grabbed the bot's tail and tore it off. Then he scooped up the bot's body and tossed it over the railing. Without pausing, he lifted his sword and rushed at the other bots that came at them.

She watched him fight, swiveling and kicking. He was hit several times by the bots' tails, but it didn't slow him down. He just kept fighting.

More movement. She saw people tripping over themselves, scrambling in all directions, and spotted another wave of bots pouring down the stairs above them. Soon, they'd be overrun.

She straightened and lifted her knife, her belly clenching.

"For honor and freedom," a deep voice roared from nearby.

"For honor and freedom!" came the shouts of several answering voices.

Sage swiveled. A muscled man with a black eye patch and a cloak of the darkest black was sprinting toward them.

A flash of relief flooded her.

Galen's gladiators were right behind him. Sage took a second to take them all in. Raiden—with his tattoos and blood-red cloak. Harper from Earth, wearing scarred fighting leathers and holding twin swords. The huge Thorin, swinging a giant axe. The tall Saff with dark hair in braids and her net in hand. Right beside her was her muscled, dark-skinned human mate, Blaine. Behind them came serious, focused Kace, and the handsome Lore, whose arm was coated in flames. Tough, muscled Nero brought up the rear, holding a giant sword in his hands, and beside him was the blue-skinned, tattooed warrior, Vek.

The House of Galen.

The gladiators crashed into the bots, weapons swinging.

Sage backed up, smiling darkly. The Edull's ugly robots were going *down*.

A flash of movement.

Something crashed into her chest.

She fell back, landing hard on the stone. A lizard bot gripped her shirt, staring down at her.

Damn, it was so heavy. She saw its tail swing, aimed right at her face. She threw her hands up. *Shit.*

It never connected.

Acton gripped the bot with his cybernetic arms. He crunched the construct between his hands, then tossed the remnants aside.

He yanked her into his arms.

"Oh, God." She clung to him.

"You're okay," Acton murmured.

She raised her head and sucked in a breath. The bots were all destroyed, remnants littering the arena. She watched Galen skewer the last one with his sword, then wrench the blade back out.

"Are you all right?" Acton asked.

She nodded, then she looked at him. He had bruises forming all over him, from where the heavy tails of the bots had struck.

"Oh, Acton." She gently touched one black mark.

"It's nothing."

It wasn't nothing to her. She pulled him closer and pressed her face to his chest. She held him tight.

"We have to stop the Edull," she whispered.

"We will."

"SAGE, I DO *NOT* TAKE BATHS."

Acton watched Sage fiddle with the faucet in his bathroom. Water flowed into the tub.

"You do today." She paused. "Will soaking in water damage your implants?"

"No. But I don't lie around in water. Ever."

Ignoring him, she shifted closer, fingering the fading bruises on his abdomen. "Avarn said it would be good for your bruising. Then I can put more med gel on you."

Acton frowned. The healer had almost been gleeful while he'd been giving Sage orders on how to care for Acton.

"I don't take baths," he tried again.

"Clothes off, cyborg," she ordered. "In you go."

He figured this was her paramedic voice. He didn't move. Then her fingers grabbed the waistband of his leathers and started opening them.

Her jaw was set in a hard line. He remembered how she'd looked when she'd been helping the injured at the Corsair Caravan. It had calmed her. Looking after others helped steady her.

With a sigh, he started to undress. He shucked his trousers and pulled his harness off. Then he climbed into the large stone tub that he'd never used.

He turned, and saw that Sage's gaze was glued to his buttocks, her cheeks pink.

"Sage?"

"Huh?" She shook herself and sat on the edge of the tub. "Sorry, got a bit distracted."

Acton scowled and sank into the water.

She lifted a cloth, dipped it in the water, then wrung it out. She started washing his shoulders. "How is it?"

"Wet."

She giggled. It was the first time he'd heard such a sound of pure joy from her. He let his gaze drift over her. She looked fine after the attack. The House of Galen and the House of Rone, along with several of their allies, were working to clean up the arena and help the injured.

To say that the imperators were angry at the Edull incursion in the arena was an understatement. The Edull would regret their actions.

But right now, Sage's smile took all his attention. For the first time, it looked real, not forced. He reached up and gripped her chin. "You aren't cold inside anymore."

She shook her head. "That's thanks to you."

"No. You are finding your place here, and searching for your crew members gives you purpose."

"True, but you're a part of it as well." She tilted her chin. "You aren't cold inside anymore, either."

No, Acton could no longer deny that this woman had broken down so many barriers inside him. He was definitely relearning how to feel.

"I believe I had a quick temper as a young man," he said.

Sadness flitted across her face. "I'm sorry you don't remember much of that time, or your family."

"I recall fields and crops. I remember running through them, with people who must have been my siblings."

"It was wrong that you were taken." Her fingers stroked down his arm.

"We can't change our pasts. The Metathim were harsh." Memories of all his missions cascaded through him. All the fights, the battles he'd been forced into, the pain, the people he'd killed. He released a breath. "But I'm free now. I have been for a long time."

"How did you get free?"

"We were on our way back from a mission. Our starship crashed here on Carthago, and many of my fellow cyborgs were killed or injured." He remembered the pained moans. A distress call had been sent, but before the recovery ship arrived, Magnus appeared. "Magnus found us."

Sage let her fingers brush the water. "And he was mad?"

Acton nodded. "He was once part of a military cyborg program similar to mine. We had enhancements forced on us, and were sent on mission after endless mission. He offered us sanctuary."

"You took it."

"I was damaged, but I saw the chance to finally escape. Some stayed, others left."

"And the Metathim?"

"They came." His lips moved. "They were not happy about losing any of their investments. They were met with resistance from the House of Rone. They left."

She leaned her head on his shoulder. "I'm glad."

She rubbed against him. Her thin shirt was wet, it was clinging to the outlines of her breasts.

When she noticed the direction of his gaze, she smiled. That smile was real, too, and all for him.

Suddenly, he needed her closer. He tugged her into the bath, and, with a squeak, she landed with a splash.

"Acton!"

He reached down and dragged the wet fabric over her head.

Then he lowered his head. She was the one who closed the last whisper of space between them, her mouth on his. She kissed him deeply, moving to straddle his body. He clamped his hands on her hips and heard her sweet moan.

He lifted her and slid his mouth over one breast. He'd discovered he really loved her breasts.

Her hand slid into his hair. "Oh, that's so good."

Soon, she was rubbing herself against him, and his cock was throbbing. It wasn't quite as overwhelming as before, but it was still mind-blowing.

"Acton." A breathy cry.

He brought his hand down and then tore her trousers off.

"You can't keep destroying my clothes," she complained.

He slid his hand between her legs, water splashing around them. As he stroked her, her head fell back.

"Okay, maybe you can." Then her gaze met his and it was full of fire. "Do you want to make love to me, Acton?"

"Yes." His voice was guttural.

Her hands reached between their bodies and circled his cock. He was as hard as stone.

She stroked him. "Do you want to be inside me?"

The voice of a temptress. His body jerked. "*Yes.*"

She kissed him again, biting his bottom lip. He sucked in a harsh breath.

"I want you inside me, Acton. So, so much."

He let out a shaky breath, blood roaring in his ears.

Her hands moved up his chest. "You okay? It's not too much?"

He managed a nod.

"I love the feel of you," she whispered. "Hard, soft, warm, cool. All the contrasts."

"I love your body, Sage. Small, pretty, soft."

He slid his hands around her, gripping the curves of her buttocks. He rubbed her against him, and then he groaned, the sensation so raw and powerful.

Sage gripped his cock, nestling the head of it between her folds.

It felt like time paused. The air rushed out of him. "Sage."

"Just feel, Acton. Feel me sinking down on you, taking you inside me." She moved her body down and moaned, biting her lip. "I can feel my body stretching to take you."

He felt it all. He felt the sweet clutch of her warmth, felt the way her body accommodated his. Then there was only the slick heat and tightness of her.

She moved down until they were joined. There was no Acton or Sage, just them, together.

She swung her hips in a circle and rose up.

He groaned. "So tight."

"Feel good?"

His fingers dug into her ass. "Yes."

Then she started riding him, rocking hard. Distantly, he heard the splash of water, but he didn't give a *drak* about it.

"Help me, Acton," she panted. "Help me fuck you."

He gripped her hips harder, and drove her up and

down on his cock.

He crashed his mouth onto hers, tongues plunging and tangling. They ground against each other wildly.

He needed more.

Acton surged out of the water, holding her tight. She wound her legs around him, and he kept her riding his cock.

He closed the distance to the bed and lowered them down, not caring at all that they were both wet. He surged inside her.

"Yes." She arched her body.

Following instinct, he hammered inside her. Wild need was twisting inside him, and he thrust hard, sliding a hand between them. He stroked where they joined, amazed at the way her body could fit him. He moved his thumb, touching her clit.

"Yes! Touch me. Make me come."

She was so slippery, and he returned to that tantalizing nub. He rubbed it and then felt her body clench on his cock, pulsing rhythmically.

"Come for me, Sage," he demanded.

She screamed, and Acton kept plunging inside her.

Then his own pleasure slammed into him.

It was incandescent, making his body shake. He groaned her name.

Wave after wave of intense emotion crashed into him.

"Sage." He could barely believe that the gritty voice was his. "*Sage.*"

Just her name. The one thing that meant everything to him.

CHAPTER THIRTEEN

S age woke to a cool hand stroking her belly.
　　　She opened her eyes and saw Acton's face—absorbed, focused on her stomach.

Okay, any man who looked at her *belly* like it was the greatest wonder in the universe was a keeper. Her heart did a little jig in her chest. This man, this cyborg, was *hers*. Hers to hold, to kiss, to love.

She felt that little tingle of fear again but she squashed it. She wasn't her mother. She refused to believe the worst in everyone.

His gaze met hers.

"Hey, there," she said.

"Good morning."

There was that crisp, cool voice she loved.

"I would like to make love to you again," he said in a serious tone.

Her breath hitched. "Okay. I have absolutely no problem with that."

He kissed her—softly, sweetly.

She made a humming noise and then he moved over her. She wrapped her arms and legs around him. His mouth traveled down her neck, his hands stroking her. She loved the way he watched and listened to her, learning what she liked best.

His mouth found a sensitive spot below her ear. Oh, she could get so lost in him.

She kissed him again, playing with his tongue. He made a harsh sound of need, his hands moving lower and pushing her legs apart.

His hard cock brushed against her, and they both groaned.

"Tell me that you want me, Sage."

She looked into his eyes. There was nothing cool about him now. His eyes were awash with heated emotion.

"I want you," she said.

His hard cock slid inside her and his powerful body shuddered. She ran her nails down his back, urging him on. As he thrust inside her, he moved a hand between them and thumbed her clit.

Sage came, his name torn from her lips. So much intense pleasure swamped her.

He groaned, long and low, his own release taking him.

In the aftermath, they snuggled together, both panting. They shared a slow, easy kiss.

Then he stiffened, a faraway look appearing in his eye.

Frowning, she sat up.

"Acknowledged," he murmured.

She realized he'd received a message. "What?"

His expression turned serious. "Magnus has narrowed down the possible location of the lake."

Sage gasped and scrambled out of the bed. "Hurry." She yanked on her clothes, and he watched her dress. "Acton, move it."

When he moved to get fresh clothing, she got side-tracked by his magnificent body. She paused, just staring at him.

"Sage?"

She shook her head. "You have the most biteable ass in the galaxy."

He blinked, then he smiled. God, she loved his smile almost as much as his ass. Forcing herself to focus, she braided her hair.

They hurried down to Magnus' office. When they entered the room, the serious atmosphere and palpable tension almost smacked her in the face. None of the cyborgs were smiling.

But as Quinn looked at Acton and Sage, the woman's lips quirked.

"Acton, you have a hickey," Quinn said gleefully.

Acton frowned. "A what?"

"A bruise on your neck. Usually from someone's mouth."

Sage blushed.

"Sage did it," Acton said.

Gasping, she smacked his arm.

"What? I liked it. Receiving it was very pleasurable."

Mace grunted and Jax grinned. Magnus' eyes were alight, and Toren averted his gaze to look at the ceiling.

Quinn was struggling not to laugh.

"God, I wish the ground would just swallow me up," Sage muttered.

Acton wrapped his arm around her. "You don't wish people to know that we—?"

"Shush." She pressed a hand to his mouth. "That's private. Just between you and me."

Understanding flashed in his eyes and he nodded.

She looked at the others. "He's still getting the hang of this whole emotions thing."

Magnus cleared his throat. "So, we knew the location of the red dunes. From there, Rillian's pilots have run some aerial searches and found the Stone Sea of Suffering."

All humor slid from Sage and she twisted her hands together.

Images appeared on the screen on the wall. Aerial shots of the desert that displayed dunes of the deepest-red sand.

Then Sage spotted the plain, filled with rock formations. "Oh, wow."

"This is the Stone Sea of Suffering," Magnus said.

"Who comes up with these names?" Quinn muttered.

The formations were all sharp, pointed, spears of rock. Some formed arches, others looked like empty tree branches, and the rest arrowed toward the heavens.

Then, a single image near the edge of the stone sea appeared.

Sage sucked in a breath.

Two sharp blades of rocks speared diagonally at each other...looking exactly like crossed daggers.

"The daggers," she murmured.

"And the lake?" Acton asked.

"There is no sign of any bodies of water," Magnus said.

Sage deflated. "Nothing?"

"No," the imperator said. "I suggest we go and take a look around."

Sage straightened. "I want to come."

Acton stiffened. "It will be dangerous—"

"I don't care," she said.

"On our last trip to the desert, the Edull attacked. You were almost hurt."

She pressed her hands to his chest and felt his heart hammering hard. "Acton, take some deep breaths."

"I...feel too much." A muscle ticked in his jaw. "Anger, fear."

"Welcome to the club," Mace grumbled.

"Deep breaths," she said again.

Acton let out a shuddering breath. "I want you safe."

She leaned into him. "And I will be, because you'll be with me."

"Sage has earned the right to come," Magnus said.

Acton didn't look happy, but he finally gave her a nod.

"When do we leave?" she asked.

"As soon as we're ready," Magnus replied.

Sage was swept into a whirlwind of preparation. Before she knew it, she was wearing desert clothes and heading into the center of the Kor Magna Arena.

Around her, the cyborgs were all prepped and armed. Quinn had refused to stay behind this time. She'd argued with Jax, and the cyborg had lost, big time. She marched ahead of him, wearing fighting leathers, her staff on her back.

It was strange being in the arena when it was empty and dimly lit, its stands devoid of people. The air was still, and the place eerily silent. She could see a repair team working in the stands, repairing damage from the Edull attack.

"Will the attack affect the fights?" she asked. "Keep the spectators away?"

Acton shook his head. "They come for the blood and many are rabid fans. Footage of the attack is already being streamed across the city. Plus, the imperators have offered free tickets and the possibility of some exhibition matches."

"Exhibition matches?"

"Friendly fights to show off new weapons and skills." He glanced at her. "And cyborgs are allowed to fight as well."

A second later, a ship appeared above the walls, hovering in the sky. It was sleek and silver.

It landed with a rush of air, kicking up sand. Sage lifted an arm to shield her face.

The side door opened and the pilot appeared.

It was Rillian.

The handsome, elegant owner of the Dark Nebula Casino nodded at them. He wore tailored combat pants and a fitted, white shirt that was open at the throat, showing a triangle of bronze skin. His eyes were a fascinating, liquid silver.

"We weren't expecting you," Magnus said.

"I decided I didn't want another of my ships crashed." The casino owner shot a pointed look at Quinn.

The woman's nose wrinkled. "It was an *emergency* landing. And I said I was sorry."

But despite his words, Rillian didn't seem concerned. He waved them aboard.

Sage followed the others into the ship, and Acton showed her to one of the wide, plush seats.

Memories tickled at the edge of her mind. She had vague memories of this ship, or one just like it. Nerves cramped her belly. The last time she'd been on a ship like this, she'd been newly rescued and barely conscious.

Acton had held her then, and she remembered a sense of strong, steady arms.

"Everyone strapped in?" Rillian called from the cockpit.

After Magnus had replied in the affirmative, the ship lifted off.

Once they were airborne and flying out over the city, Quinn unbuckled and headed into the cockpit. Sage could hear her asking Rillian questions.

In the back, the cyborgs were quiet. Sage shifted on her seat, a few sensitive aches between her legs reminding her of what she and Acton had been doing. But right now, she couldn't think of that. The minutes ticked by, turning into hours. As time blurred, Sage's nerves tightened.

Her head was wracked with all the things that could be happening to Simone and Grace. *God, please be okay.*

Finally, after what felt like forever, Rillian announced that they'd be landing.

The casino owner was a very good pilot, and the landing was smooth.

Magnus rose. "How's the ship holding up?"

"Fine," Rillian replied. "Some damage to the engines, but the auto-repair system is already hard at work. With all these trips to the desert, my engineers have been able to adjust to the damage the sand does. With each trip, our capabilities increase."

The casino owner touched the controls on the door. When the side door opened, a blast of hot, dry air hit them.

Magnus was the first off.

Sage followed the others off the ship, the scorching, desert suns beating down on them. Her throat tightened.

As she stared at the empty, desert horizon, she knew they were close to the Edull. To the aliens who'd hurt her without blinking an eye.

On this mission, it was likely that she'd see some of her captors again.

"Sage?"

She looked up at Acton. His direct gaze was focused on her, a glint of concern in his eyes.

"I'm ready." She tossed her shoulders back, wrapping her scarf over her head. She stared at the vast red dunes in the distance. "Let's go and find Simone and Grace."

RILLIAN SET the high-tech security system on the ship, a blue shimmer of energy gleaming across the hull.

"I'm coming with you," he said.

Magnus eyed the man for a moment, then nodded. Acton knew Rillian was a good addition to their group. Even while he was wearing black combat gear, the casino owner still managed to look elegant, but he was also bonded to a powerful alien symbiont that gave him incredible strength.

They moved off at a steady pace, and he watched the sand turn a deeper shade of red. One dune rose up around them, large and imposing.

As they neared the crest of the dune, Acton glanced at Sage.

Her face was flushed, but she was keeping up. She was determined to save her fellow humans.

The same way she was determined to drag him into a real life.

She looked his way and smiled.

Then she reached out and took his hand, her fingers twining with his cybernetic ones, holding on tight. Flesh mixed with metal, but it didn't matter that they were different, they were linked.

Acton felt his heart fill with warmth, the organ coming back to life. He shook his head. He was well aware that his heart functioned perfectly, pumping blood around his body. Sage clearly was having a fanciful effect on him.

They crested the dune, and Sage gasped.

Acton stared at the rock formations down below.

The Stone Sea of Suffering.

He scanned around, using his system scanners to check the area. "I'm not detecting any water."

Sage bit her lip, and they kept trekking. Soon, he saw clouds building up ahead above the formations.

There had to be water here somewhere.

Slowly, the dunes got smaller, and they hit what appeared to be a large, white, rocky plain. The formations speared up around them, casting shadows across the ground.

They trekked on until the daggers appeared, the crossed rocks looming above them.

They stopped by the rock formation, and Sage idly stroked the twisted rock. "Where is the damn lake?"

"Spread out," Magnus ordered. "Look around."

Acton paused, scanning around again. All he detected was rock and sand.

Sage kicked at the ground, moving away from him. She moved into a small clearing between the rocks.

"Look at this." She crouched down, brushing her hand on the hard surface.

He moved closer, and on the ground, he spotted hexagonal formations that looked almost like tiles.

"These remind me of the Giant's Causeway on Earth," she said. "Pillars made when molten rock came up through softer rock. They're really beautiful." She rose and walked out across the hexagonal shapes. "Looks like they go on for a long way."

But it didn't help them find any hidden lakes.

She stopped again and crouched. Her brow creased. "Acton." She brushed some salt away.

He saw what she was looking at. There was a fossil in the rock. A tiny skeleton, no bigger than Sage's hand.

The skeleton looked like it had been aquatic.

"This looks like the fossil of a fish." She scanned the plain. "There was a lake here, once upon a time."

"Acton." Magnus' deep voice came through Acton's internal comms.

Acton tilted his head. "Here, Magnus. Anything?"

"No. You?"

"Sage found a small fossil of some aquatic animal. There's no telling the age."

"Keep searching."

Sage moved away, her gaze glued to the ground. Acton saw her stumble.

"Sage?"

She spun, her face flaring with panic. "One of the hexagons crumbled beneath my foot."

He stiffened. "Don't move."

"There's a hole." She leaned over, peering downward. "There's something *under* here."

Acton took a step closer, and a puff of dust rose up to Sage's left. Another hexagon had fallen in.

What the drak?

Sage yelped. Around her, more hexagons were dropping away.

Acton's pulse picked up speed. "Sage, come to me—"

She took one step and lifted her head. Their gazes met.

"Acton!" The ground beneath her dropped away and she fell.

One second, she was there, the next she was gone.

"Magnus! Sage just fell. The ground's caving in."

"We're coming, Acton. Wait for us!"

It felt like acid was burning inside him. Acton sprinted toward where Sage had disappeared, trying to think through the rush of emotions.

Right now, Sage needed him cool-headed.

A huge hole, the size of a transport, had opened up in the ground. Looking down, all he could see was darkness.

No.

He had to get to Sage. He wasn't going to wait for the others.

He jumped feet first after her, plummeting downward.

He dropped for a long time, then suddenly he hit water with a splash, sinking deep. He kicked hard to reach the surface.

"Acton!"

He spotted Sage nearby, her wet hair stuck to her head. She was treading water.

Acton grabbed her, holding her tight.

"I'm okay." She beamed at him. "And I found the lake."

He turned. Light streamed in from the hole above, illuminating the dark water around them. They were in the center of an underground lake that spread out around them. He couldn't see anything except a small sandbank nearby and water—still and dark.

CHAPTER FOURTEEN

A cton towed Sage to the sandbank.
They both collapsed there, catching their
breath. The water was surprisingly cool, and she
shivered.

But she was just damn glad the sand was there.

Acton was talking to Magnus.

"We're okay. Yes, the lake's deep and large.
Acknowledged."

He turned to look at her. "The others are coming."

They'd found the lake. Excitement fizzed through
Sage like soda bubbles.

A second later, a big body arrowed down from above.
It splashed into the water like a missile. Magnus.

The flap of a red cloak. Jax landed in the water.

One by one, the others followed.

The House of Rone cyborgs, Rillian, and Quinn all
swam over to the sandbank.

"Okay?" Quinn asked.

Sage nodded.

"My scanners aren't giving clear readings," Acton said.

Magnus frowned. "I'm detecting *dantane* in the rock. The mineral will distort our scanners and comms." The imperator looked around the gloom. "I am detecting what looks like a large network of tunnels nearby." He pointed, and Sage could just barely make out a distant shoreline. Maybe.

"Time for a swim," Jax said.

Toren and Acton flicked on small lights on their cybernetic implants. They all started across the water. Sage used some breaststroke, kicking hard. While aboard the *Helios*, swimming was something she'd missed.

They were halfway across when Rillian stopped, treading water. A frown marred the man's handsome face.

"Rillian?" Magnus asked.

"My symbiont is...unsettled."

There was a splash in the water nearby, a ripple breaking the smooth surface.

Sage's heart stopped for a moment. *Oh, no.*

"There's something in the water," Quinn whispered.

"Swim," Magnus ordered.

They all moved, cutting through the water as fast as they could. More ripples broke out, and Sage spotted a dark body that briefly rose to the surface for a moment.

Her gut clenched, primal fear moving through her.

Acton's arm brushed hers. "Keep going. I won't let anything hurt you."

There were more splashes all around them. Jeez, whatever they were, there were a lot of them.

"They're surrounding us," Mace growled.

"What the hell are they?" Quinn asked.

Suddenly, Toren cursed. Something yanked the cyborg under the water.

As Toren disappeared, Sage cried out. Jax dove into the water and Quinn drew a knife.

There was a loud splash behind them, and they all spun.

That's when Sage got a good view of one of the creatures.

Her breath caught in her throat. They were shark-like *robots*. They were made of scrap metal, with sinuous bodies, and powerful tails covered in spikes.

And gleaming metal fangs.

Oh, fuck.

"Go!" Acton yelled.

Toren and Jax burst out of the water, heaving in air.

One of the shark bots rose up, arrowing toward Quinn. As it neared, she dodged to the side and stabbed at it with her knife.

It thrashed around, jaws snapping at the woman. It broke free, turned in a quick circle, and rushed back at her again.

Jax was swimming toward Quinn as fast as he could. She stabbed at the bot again, and one of its neon eyes flared, then winked out.

But it snapped its jaws again, and Quinn cried out.

It had her shoulder. It thrashed, throwing her around. Blood was spreading in the water.

Jax roared and slammed into the side of the shark. It

let Quinn go, and with an enraged noise, Jax rammed his fist into the metal, punching a hole into it.

The shark bot floundered.

More bots swam in, converging on them. All the cyborgs turned to face them. Mace rammed into one, Toren fired his weapon, and Magnus charged through the water.

Fighting her terror, Sage felt something brush her leg.

She spun, kicking. Acton moved closer, shoving his arms into the water.

"I've got it," he said, between gritted teeth.

Sage looked up and saw a pale-faced Quinn being held by Jax.

"I'll help her." Sage took the woman's weight. Acton tread water, clearly not wanting to leave them unprotected. "I've got her. Go."

Reluctantly, Acton and Jax turned back to the fight.

Kicking to stay above the water, Sage held on tight to Quinn. "How you doing, Quinn?"

"Fine." A grimace crossed her face.

"As soon as we get to shore, I'll patch you up." Sage studied the jagged, bleeding wound on Quinn's shoulder. "It doesn't look too deep."

"Always been afraid of sharks," the tough woman said.

Sage snorted. "I could tell. Especially when you were stabbing that shark bot with a knife."

Quinn managed a smile.

The cyborgs were still fighting, the bots thrashing in the water. She watched Magnus climb on top of one shark, punching it with his cybernetic arm.

Mace grabbed the tail of another bot, spun it around, and threw it out across the water.

Toren was hurt, barely staying above the water, but his weapon was still firing.

Acton used his cybernetic powers, a shark bot rising up out of the water.

Sage got a good look at the thing and a shiver worked through her. The ugly creation was built for death.

"Fucking Edull," Sage said.

"But look at our cyborgs," Quinn said. "Badass."

Sage couldn't help but smile. They sure were.

Acton swam back to them. "Come on. We need to get to the other side." Acton gripped Sage's arm, and Jax appeared to help Quinn.

Toren was bleeding, a trail of blood in the water behind him. He didn't look like he was doing very well. Magnus and Rillian moved up on either side of the injured cyborg, and propelled him through the water.

Finally, they dragged themselves up onto a rocky beach.

Sage pushed up on her hands and knees, giving herself two seconds to suck in some breath. Then she crawled to Quinn and yanked a small first aid kit off her belt. She opened the pack and pulled out some med gel and bandages.

Opening Quinn's shirt, she squirted the blue gel onto the wound, then pressed the adhesives to Quinn's skin. The bandages sucked onto the wound and stopped the bleeding. Finding a pressure injector, she gave Quinn a quick shot of painkillers.

"Thanks, Sage," Jax said.

"Sage," Acton said.

She turned and saw Toren sprawled on his back. He had several bite marks on his legs and a terrible wound on his stomach. She guessed he'd lost lots of blood.

"Hey." Sage dropped down beside the injured cyborg.

"My systems have slowed the bleeding." His voice was a little slurred. His blond hair looked shades darker now that it was wet.

Sage cracked open her kit and pulled out the med gel. She started squeezing it into the worst of his wounds. He had a nasty scratch on his face, and she smoothed some gel over it.

"Hey? You still with me?"

He nodded and blinked slowly. He really had beautiful eyes. They were a brilliant blue, ringed by silver.

"Don't stare at me too hard," Toren murmured. "I'm pretty sure Acton can feel jealousy now."

She smiled at the cyborg. He had some hidden charm, this one.

As she worked on him, she glanced up. She saw Magnus, Acton, and the others looking at the entrances to the tunnels and talking quietly.

She didn't look forward to seeing what else the Edull had hidden in the darkness.

She pressed some bandages on Toren's injuries. "You're all done. Won't be long, and you'll be as good as new."

"And I didn't even need an oil change."

She snorted. "Is that cyborg humor?"

Toren schooled his face. "Acton would tell you that cyborgs don't have a sense of humor."

"I think you guys are good at pretending." Rising, she went back to the water's edge to wash the blood off her hands.

She peered out at the lake in awe once more. It was smooth as glass.

She dipped her fingers in the water. Suddenly, a shark bot reared up out of the water.

Teeth snapped and gripped her shirt. Sage screamed.

"Sage!" Acton's yell.

His voice was the last thing she heard before she was dragged beneath the surface.

RAW PANIC ROCKETED THROUGH ACTON.

He watched Sage disappear under the water. Pain like he'd never known before hit him hard.

Sage.

He sprinted for the water, hearing the shouts of the others behind him.

But he couldn't make sense of them over the roar in his ears. Without pausing, he dived into the water.

He followed the ripple of bubbles, kicking as hard as he could, pushing for every ounce of power he had. He enhanced his vision to see better through the dark water.

He made good distance, and in the gloom, he saw the outline of the shark and Sage appear. She was struggling, hammering her fists against the robot.

The bot was racing across the lake. Acton kicked

harder as he chased them. He got close enough to grab the shark's tail.

Spikes scraped his metal skin, but he held on tight. The bot shook its tail wildly, and Acton was thrown about. He gritted his teeth and held on. He used his other hand to punch the bot, and felt the metal dent.

Still caught in the shark's grip, Sage's movements were slowing. She was running out of air.

Acton's cybernetic systems could compensate for the lack of air. He wouldn't need it for a much longer time than she did.

He punched the shark again.

The tail shook again and he almost lost his grip.

The bot picked up speed, racing toward the rock wall.

Drak. They were going to smash right into it. Acton's pulse spiked.

But then, the shark dove, and darted into a tunnel that Acton could barely see. They barreled through the water-filled tunnel, Acton's body scraping against the wall. The tunnel wasn't very wide.

Drak, he had to get Sage free.

She was still fighting, but her movements were sluggish. Her hair had slipped free of its tie, the copper strands trailing behind her like a wave.

Hold on, Sage. I'll get you.

Gripping on, he climbed up the robot and punched into its side. He punched again.

At that moment, Sage went limp, hanging in the bot's jaws like a rag.

No!

Using all his strength, Acton punched through the shark's gut.

The bot jerked. He poured his cybernetic power into the bot, scrambling its insides.

It went into a wild, frenzied thrashing.

Sage was jerked around, and one of Acton's hands slipped off the metal. *No.*

With grim determination, he slammed his palm down on a spike. It speared through his palm and his systems blocked the pain. He held on. Sage wouldn't give up on him, and he wasn't giving up on her.

Suddenly, the shark went still. It started sinking toward the bottom of the tunnel. Acton yanked his hand free of the spike and kicked.

He grabbed Sage.

Forward or back? He needed to get her air as soon as he could, and they'd come a long way into the tunnel.

She wasn't moving. Panic and other emotions churned inside him. He couldn't think or calculate the odds.

He made a decision. Kicking hard, he swam forward, powering through the water.

He wound through the tunnel. *Come on.* They needed to surface. Sage was a tiny, limp weight in his arms, and she needed air. He needed to save her.

Then, he saw a glimmer of light above him.

He looked up. There was a tunnel above them. Changing direction, he rocketed upward. He kicked hard, with all the energy he had.

Acton broke the surface of the water. His lungs kicked in, dragging in air.

Lifting Sage into his arms, he staggered onto a rocky shore in a small cavern. The walls were lined with a glittering substance that gave off light. A tunnel entrance yawned in the darkness.

He laid Sage on the ground.

She was so still, so pale. Her hair was stuck to her cheeks and he pushed it back.

Tilting her head back, he pressed his mouth over hers and breathed.

Nothing.

He breathed into her. Again. Again.

Her chest didn't move.

"Sage." His voice was a broken sound.

She'd come into his life, dug under his skin and his enhancements. He didn't want a life without her.

He breathed again, cupping her pale, cool cheeks.

"Sage, you *have* to live. I can't do this without you."

Still nothing.

Again, pain rushed through him. He thumped her chest.

"You can't bring me back to life and then leave me." He pressed his lips to hers, pain tearing him apart.

And then she jerked.

He sat up and helped her rise. She coughed, rolling onto her side and vomiting up water.

Then she sagged against him. "Acton?"

He wrapped his arms around her, and for the first time since he was a child, tears coursed down his cheeks.

CHAPTER FIFTEEN

Sage stayed snuggled in Acton's arms for several long moments. She liked it there.

"Magnus, respond." Acton shook his head. "No contact."

She worried her bottom lip. So, for now, they were on their own. They were both wet and shaken, but they were alive.

Acton was holding her tight. Really tight. He seemed to need the contact more than she did.

He stroked her hair and she turned into him, pressing her cheek to his skin. "I'm okay, thanks to you."

"I never, *ever* want to do that again." His voice was drenched with emotion.

Oh, God, this man, this cyborg, had turned her inside out in such a short time. She pressed her lips to his and kissed him—long and deep.

Eventually, he sighed. "We should get moving and find the others."

She nodded, rising a little unsteadily. She guessed it

159

wasn't a huge surprise that being almost drowned and killed by a robot shark left a girl a little unsettled. Acton watched her like a hawk, so she locked her knees.

She huffed out a breath. "I'm okay. I promise."

He gave her another long look, then nodded. Grabbing her hand, he led her into the tunnel. A narrow beam of light clicked on from one of Acton's cybernetic arms.

The rock walls were bare, showing no signs of occupation.

"Do you think the Edull made these?" she asked.

"It looks like a natural system, but I can see that it's been enhanced in places."

A shiver worked up her spine. The Edull were here, somewhere.

And that might mean Simone and Grace were too.

Periodically, Acton tried to make contact with the others. But each time, his jaw tightened, and he shook his head.

"The *dantane* in the rock is still interrupting our communications."

"We'll find them."

Suddenly, Acton paused and gripped her arm. He stared deep into the tunnel ahead.

"What is it?" she whispered.

"I hear noises. Voices."

Her pulse jumped. Acton motioned her back behind him, and they quietly crept forward.

Moments later, the tunnel ended at a narrow ledge. A huge cavern yawned ahead of them. She heard clanking and hissing.

Sage held her breath and Acton pulled her down. She shimmied on her belly and peered over the edge.

She sucked in a harsh breath.

Edull. Everywhere. She stared down at the aliens moving below. They all wore dark robes and ugly, black masks over their faces. All around, the clanking of metal echoed off the rock walls—tools striking metal, equipment working and chugging. In some places, sparks sprayed into the air.

The Edull had rows of workbenches and construction lines set up. Boxes and containers overflowing with scrap metal were stacked all over the place.

They were building bots of all shapes and sizes.

Sage felt as though a huge rock were lodged in her throat. A gurgling sound nearby caught her ear, and she glanced over to see clear pipes filled with water that had clearly come from the underground lake running along the rocky walls.

She followed the lines down to the floor of the cavern, and saw several large vats of water. As she watched, a large bot—its metal surface glowing red-hot—was lowered into the water. There was a hiss of steam as hot metal met the liquid.

So many dangerous bots being created. She tried to pull air into her tight chest.

"Do you think they know the House of Rone is here?" she whispered.

Acton stared into the cavern. "I don't think so. The shark bots did not appear to have any communications."

She scanned the rest of the cavern, and then she felt Acton stiffen.

He was showing his emotions so much more freely now. She tore her eyes off his taut face, and followed his gaze.

Then she saw the cells.

A cry tried to escape, but she bit her lip. Her hand groped for his. Strong metal fingers closed on hers.

There was a long row of cells along one of the rock walls. *So many.*

She could see people inside the cages, some sitting, some huddled, some with their hands wrapped around the metal bars.

Sage also saw a lot of smaller figures in the cells. *Children.* Her belly cramped painfully.

"Acton." A broken whisper.

He pulled her closer to his side.

"The Edull are cold, unforgiving monsters," she said.

"That's what some people say about cyborgs."

"Well, some people are idiots, and don't know what they're talking about." She paused. "We need to get down there."

He nodded and pressed a quick kiss to her forehead. "I've managed a partial scan of the nearby tunnels. There's a way down." He pulled her away from the edge. "You'll do everything I say? So I can keep you safe?"

She nodded.

"If I tell you to run, you'll run?"

"I will." But she wouldn't promise to leave. She wouldn't abandon a child, or him.

Acton pulled back into the shadowed tunnel. "Let's go."

ACTON REALLY WISHED he could contact the others.

He didn't want to take Sage down to that cavern and into more danger. He blew out a breath. But his human was brave. Not fearless—he knew she was afraid—but she'd act anyway to save others. That was true bravery.

He pulled her through the tunnels, and soon they descended downward. At the bottom, the sounds of construction were louder, and he could feel the heat of the furnaces. They paused, their backs pressed to the rock wall.

Acton peeked around the edge of the rock. They weren't far from the cells. There were a few Edull guards, but not too many. They clearly felt they were safe here, hidden in their tunnels beneath the sand.

One Edull guard passed by close to their tunnel entrance, and Acton pulled back, holding Sage to the wall. She glared at the Edull.

As the alien wandered closer, Acton darted out and grabbed him. The man jerked in surprise, but with one twist of his cybernetic arms, Acton broke the Edull's neck.

He dragged the body back into the dark of the tunnel. Over the alien's body, he met Sage's gaze. He half expected to see horror, but she just nodded, a resolved, no-nonsense look in her eyes.

Acton nodded his head in return, and together, they darted out of the tunnel. They ducked behind a stack of boxes. The crates were overflowing with metal scrap.

He pointed and Sage nodded. Keeping low, they ran to the next set of boxes.

They were close to one of the construction lines, and Sage muffled a gasp. Up close, the bots were huge and monstrous. Each one was a different design—some with tracks, some with wheels, others with multiple legs.

All of them included lots of weapons.

Another Edull came close, his robes flapping around his body. Acton heard the alien's rasping breathing. Sinking lower, he pulled Sage down and they waited, tense.

"We need this batch of bots ready today," the Edull rasped. "They're transporting them to the battle arena tonight."

There was a muffled response from whoever he was talking with.

Battle arena? Acton looked at the huge bots. He had a very bad feeling about this.

Once the Edull was gone, he took Sage's hand and tugged her out of cover. They moved close to the cells.

They moved behind another stack of more scrap parts, but as they circled around them, they bumped straight into an Edull guard.

The alien's beady, black eyes widened, and he sucked in a shocked breath through the valve in his mask.

Drak.

Before Acton could move, Sage leaped on the Edull, taking the alien down.

"Bastard," she whispered harshly.

Drak. They had to stop him from raising the alarm. Acton went down on one knee and pressed his hands to the man's torso, keeping him pinned. He used his power to tear off the Edull's mask. The guard started to choke, clutching at his throat.

But Acton didn't let up. Finally, the Edull slumped.

Sage moved back, swallowing. "God."

Acton lifted the body and slid it inside the nearest crate, covering the Edull with scrap. Then he ducked back down. "Sage?"

She burrowed against him, her hands clutching at his skin. "I'm fine."

He let himself hold her for a second, then turned his head. His gaze fell on another stack of crates right beside them. He stiffened.

"What?" she whispered.

He just stared, not believing what he saw. She turned her head before he could stop her.

She hissed in a breath and pressed a hand to her mouth. "Are those—?"

"Yes."

These crates weren't full of metal scrap, they were filled with body parts.

Acton identified limbs, strips of flesh, hair. Sage made a gagging noise, and he pulled her face into his chest. "Breathe."

He scanned the nearby containers and confirmed that there were several boxes containing organic parts. When he looked at the closest workbenches, he saw several bots were having organic parts and organs added to their design.

He pressed his lips together. Sage was right, the Edull were monsters.

He pulled in a deep breath. "Sage, we need to free the prisoners. Now." Before they ended up being used for parts.

Her jaw was tight, but she nodded.

His woman was made of steel under her skin. They headed toward the cells, and when they reached the first one, the people inside looked at them with dull gazes.

"We're going to get you out," Sage whispered.

Acton snapped the lock off the cell door. He moved along to the next ones, doing the same. One, two, three.

"Wait until we cause a diversion," he said. "Then run for the tunnels."

Realizing the cage doors were open, a few of the people stirred.

At the next cell, Sage stilled. Acton stepped up behind her.

A young girl—in dirt-covered clothes—rose slowly. She had a fall of straight, black hair, pretty, dark eyes, and pale skin.

"Grace," Sage breathed.

The girl tilted her head, her hands clenched into fists. She nodded. "You're from the *Helios*."

Sage nodded. "We're here to get you out."

"I'm not going anywhere without my mom."

Acton almost smiled. Clearly on Earth, they bred toughness into their women young.

"We will find your mother," he said.

The girl eyed him and his enhancements. Her gaze was bold and direct. The Edull hadn't broken this young girl. She gave them a small nod.

She moved to the cell door, and Acton grabbed the lock, twisted it off—

A huge force punched into his lower back.

"Acton!" He heard Sage grunt, and then a scuffling sound. "Let me go."

Acton was hit again, and he slammed into the bars of the cage.

"Stop it," Sage yelled.

Inside, the girl was watching him, her eyes wide. He saw one of her hands clench into a fist.

Another hit to his back and pain tore through his body. His legs gave out, and he slid down the bars. He had internal damage now, and his systems were working hard to try and heal what it could.

When he turned his head, he saw several Edull. One was holding some sort of piston-driven weapon that he punched into Acton's body.

Another Edull was holding Sage. She twisted in his grip until the alien shook her and snarled.

Acton gritted his teeth. The sandsucker would regret putting his hands on her.

"They'll both be good for parts," the Edull who'd attacked him rasped. "I'm going to enjoy pulling the cyborg apart. Lock them up."

His gaze met Sage's. Her eyes were wide and panicked.

I'll get you out. I promise.

CHAPTER SIXTEEN

S age lifted her feet and kicked as hard as she could. Her anger outweighed her fear. She jerked her elbow back, and heard her Edull captor grunt.

"Leave her alone," a young voice cried.

Grace flew at the Edull, clawing at the alien's mask. The Edull's arm shot out and grabbed the girl's robes. He shoved Grace hard and she fell to the ground.

"Bastard." Sage swiveled and kicked his thigh. He staggered. She landed a punch to his face and felt a satisfying crunch.

He dropped her and she spun. Her gaze fell on Acton.

He was collapsed on the ground, not moving. Her heart leaped into her throat.

Two Edull tried to heave him up.

She had to help him.

Suddenly, a weight hit Sage from behind, and she found herself on her knees on the ground. Her arms were wrenched behind her back.

"Behave, or I'll knock you out," an Edull rasped in her ear.

She sagged and saw another Edull guard lifting Grace by the back of her clothes. The girl kicked and snarled.

The other two Edull started dragging Acton away.

"Where are you taking him?" Sage demanded.

Her captor didn't answer. She and Grace were shoved inside a cell. Sage was stripped of her gear and weapons. Grace scuttled toward the back of the cell, glaring at the Edull.

The door clanged shut, and Sage curled her fingers around the bars. She stared at Acton's lax form.

"What are you doing with him?" she yelled.

One Edull turned back, his breathing harsh. "We're going to use him for parts."

Nausea hit her, and she watched until she lost sight of Acton. A sob sat trapped in her throat.

"Are you okay?"

Sage pulled in a breath and turned to Grace. The young girl had such a pretty face, even with it streaked with dirt and lined with concern.

Sage had to be strong for this girl, who'd already been through so much. She crouched in front of Grace. "I'm okay. Are you all right?"

Grace nodded.

"Grace, I'm Sage McAlister from the *Helios*."

The girl swallowed and tears welled in her eyes. She quickly dashed them away. "It's nice to meet you, Sage. It's been kind of...lonely."

Sage reached out and hugged the girl fiercely. Grace

tensed for a second, then threw her arms around Sage, burying her face in Sage's neck.

"I'm going to get you out of here," Sage promised.

Grace shook her head. "I'm not leaving without my mom."

"We'll find her. Acton and I aren't alone, and his friends will be here soon." She sure hoped she wasn't lying.

Grace nodded.

Rising, Sage looked through the bars, chewing on her lip.

"You're worried about him," the young girl said.

"I am. He's strong and powerful, but he needs me."

And she was locked in a cell, deep in the bowels of this Edull nightmare. God, it was a terrible time to realize that she was head over heels for the cyborg.

"We need a plan." Her voice wavered, despair like acid in her chest. They were trapped, with no weapons, and no way to contact Magnus and the others.

She couldn't let the Edull win. She dropped her head in her hands. She needed to be strong for Acton, for Grace.

The girl touched Sage's shoulder. Then Grace shifted her loose sleeve and held up a thin strip of wire.

Sage frowned.

"I can pick the lock," Grace said. "I've done it before."

Sage blinked. "Really?"

The girl nodded. "I've been snooping around and sneaking out to look for my mom."

Sage smiled. "That's awesome, and very brave."

The girl gave her an answering smile. They moved to the door of the cell, and Grace slipped her slender hands through the bars and started to work on the lock.

Sage kept watch, making sure none of the guards came too close. Then she heard footsteps.

"Edull," she whispered.

They stepped back and the guard gave them a glare as he passed by.

Cautiously, they went back to work, and Grace jimmied the lock, her tongue caught between her teeth.

God, she was so young. Sage wanted to stroke her hair. She should never have been through this terrible situation. She should be in school, playing, laughing, learning.

"How old are you?" Sage asked.

"Eight."

She seemed older. "Have you seen your mom?"

A flash of sadness crossed Grace's face. "Yes. Only a glimpse. She protected me, but they separated us. She's here somewhere, though, I know it."

Sage brushed Grace's cheek gently. "We'll find her. I promise."

Click.

The lock opened. Grace and Sage grinned at each other. They quickly slipped out, closing the cell door behind them.

"That way." Grace pointed. "We need to find mom."

They quickly hurried down the line of cells. Sage peered inside each one at the bedraggled people, and felt the air of hopelessness.

So many prisoners with a terrible fate awaiting them.

Her gut churned. She wanted to rescue them all, but she couldn't risk it right now. She knew it would take too long for them to pick each of the locks, but dammit, it hurt.

They kept searching. No Simone.

Grace's face wavered, but then determination filled her. "We keep looking."

The next cell held two males. The following one held a family group. There was only one more cell.

It held a lone figure, who sat against the wall, shoulders slumped. Tangled, black hair covered the prisoner's face.

"Hey," Sage called out softly.

The woman lifted her head. Her face was badly bruised, but it was clearly Simone. The woman stiffened. "Grace?"

"Mom."

Simone shot to her feet.

"Mom!" The little girl picked at the lock, fighting to get it open, her hands shaking. Simone reached through the bars and grabbed the girl's hands.

"Baby girl."

"We've come to get you out," Grace said.

Life flared in Simone's dark eyes. "Grace." She cupped her daughter's cheeks, and two tears slid down Grace's cheeks.

"After," Sage said. "Grace, finish picking the lock. We need to move."

Grace got back to work and Sage met Simone's gaze. The other woman nodded.

Sage heard a sound. An Edull guard wandered closer, in profile to them. She tensed.

Shit. They had nowhere to hide.

Then he turned away without spotting them, and she let out a breath.

"You're from the *Helios*," Simone murmured.

"Sage McAlister. I was part of the medical team. I came to get you both out."

"You're alone?"

"My man is with me." Worry was like a punch to her belly. "The Edull took him. There are others with us, but we got separated."

The cell door clicked open. Simone pushed out of the cell and swept her daughter off her feet.

"Love you, baby girl." The woman's hands were shaking. Grace clung tightly to her mother, her face buried in Simone's neck.

"We need to find a way out," Sage said.

Simone set her daughter down and nodded.

"That way," Grace said.

But they'd only taken a few steps when an agonized groan filled the air, rising above the rattle and crash of construction.

Sage faltered. "Acton."

She swiveled, her feet moving before she thought her actions through.

"Sage—" Simone's fingers brushed her shoulder.

Another pained sound that speared Sage like a lance. She crouched behind a box and peered around the edge.

Bile filled the back of her throat.

Acton was stretched out on a bench, held in place by some torturous-looking chains. Several Edull circled him.

Grace and Simone dropped down beside her, but Sage couldn't look away from Acton.

One Edull held some sort of tool, and was digging into one of Acton's cybernetic arms.

Sage must have moved because Simone grabbed her. "You'll get yourself imprisoned or killed."

Acton's body arched and he groaned. Sage bit down on her lip.

Then the Edull set the tool down, gripped Acton's arm, and wrenched it off. Acton jerked, his roar of pain making Sage shudder.

Tears burned in her eyes. "We have to help him." She turned to Simone. "He's mine and I love him." *Oh, God.* She loved him, which left her both exhilarated and afraid. "He's suffered so much in his past, and I'm not leaving him."

When she looked back, she saw the Edull grabbing more tools.

"Okay, let's think this through." Simone turned and Sage saw the intelligence burning in the woman's eyes. "We need weapons, or something. A diversion?"

Grace's eyes lit up. "I have an idea."

The girl weaved through the crates and boxes. She led them to a pile of boxes filled with rows of bottles. The clear containers were filled with strange fluids of different colors.

"We can build a bomb," Grace announced.

Sage blinked. "What?"

The girl crouched and started studying the fluids,

picking some bottles and discarding others. "These are chemicals the Edull use."

Wide-eyed, Sage looked at Simone.

The woman gave her a slightly pained smile. "I'm a chemist. My daughter has a genius IQ, and a knack for trouble."

"Once, I blew up the science lab at school," Grace said. "Accidentally."

Simone made a humming noise.

"And I might have mixed a few of these before." Grace smiled. "They had no idea what caused the crates to explode."

Sage blew out a breath and glanced back to Acton. She could just glimpse him through the crates. His big body was shaking.

"Okay, let's build a bomb."

Grace was already mixing things together, and Simone leaned in and helped. Sage listened to the pair murmur to each other, and the fizzing sound of chemicals mixing. Every few seconds, she glanced around to make sure they weren't being spotted.

"Right, back up," Simone said.

Sage spotted some large, heavy-duty crates not too far away. She raced over to them, and dropped down behind them.

Then she watched Grace pull a device from her pocket.

A flame came out of the end of the device. The girl threw it toward the chemicals and it arched through the air.

Simone grabbed her daughter's hand, and mother and daughter ran to Sage, diving beside her.

Sage gripped her thighs. "When will—?"

Boom.

The sound was deafening. Rock and debris flew everywhere. Sage dived on top of the others and squeezed her eyes closed. *Holy. cow.*

CHAPTER SEVENTEEN

A ll Acton was aware of was pain, heat, and fire. His systems were badly damaged. He yanked on his remaining arm and legs, but while the chains clanked, he couldn't get free.

Around him, the Edull were panicking. Several were injured, and others were running to find their attackers.

Acton strained, pulling on the chains. Pain throbbed through him and he roared. The chains were designed to hold strong bots, and could easily hold cyborgs.

He flopped back on the bench, panting. Where was Sage? Was she okay? He needed to get to her.

He would not allow anyone to hurt her again.

Then suddenly, a hand ran along his shoulder, and he jolted. *Sage.* Perhaps the pain was causing him to hallucinate.

"Oh, Acton." There were tears in her eyes. She pressed something to the bleeding wound on his shoulder.

She was real. He watched her pull herself together

and turn into the no-nonsense paramedic. She dealt with his injury with efficient moves, holding some scrap of fabric she'd obviously found somewhere.

"You caused the explosion," he said.

She nodded. "I had a little help."

He turned his head, and through the flickering flames, he saw a dark-haired woman standing with the young girl, Grace.

"You can't break the chains," Grace said. "You need a key."

A key the Edull would have.

"Get out of here," Acton said. "Find Magnus and the others—"

"I'm *not* leaving you here." Sage's tone was fierce.

"Sage—"

She cupped his cheek. "No. They've already taken your arm, and they are not taking any more. You are *mine*, Acton. Mine to protect."

He stared at her face in the flickering light. "I believe I might be falling in love with you."

She sucked in a breath, her mouth dropping open. He also saw a flash of fear in her eyes.

"I will love you, always. Just as you are. I will give my life for you. I may not have lots of experience with emotion and love, but I will not be your mother, or the others who didn't treat you right."

"Be quiet." She pressed a quick kiss to his lips. "You need to work on your timing, cyborg."

When she straightened, determination was written all over her.

"First things first, we need to get you free." She

picked up one of the Edull tools, and started trying to break the chains holding him. "Grace, do you think you could pick the lock?"

The girl's eyes narrowed. "I can try."

Acton blinked at the rocky ceiling, watching the swirling smoke. He wanted them all safe, but he couldn't think of anything to say or do that would convince them to leave.

"Watch out!" Simone yelled.

Two Edull barreled out of the smoke and flames.

Sage spun, lifted the long tool in her hand, and with a cry, she ran at the aliens. She swung the tool, and the Edull dodged. She swung again and caught one in the side. He grunted and staggered back.

Simone hurtled into the other one, knocking him over. Then Grace leaped on the Edull's back, a feral look on her face.

Acton groaned, fighting his bindings. He was *drakking* helpless, forced to watch the women fight.

The Edull spun, tossing the girl off. She fell to the ground and the alien kicked her.

"Leave her alone." Sage rushed at him with her tool.

She swung high, smacking him in the head. She swung and hit him again.

The Edull blinked, then lost consciousness. He went down, knocking Sage over.

As Simone helped her up, the first Edull had risen, pulling a large knife off his belt.

"Sage!" Acton strained against his restraints.

All of a sudden, laser bolts blasted through the air,

slamming into the Edull. He dropped, and the laser ricocheted, hitting the second Edull on the ground.

Both aliens lay unmoving. Simone gasped, pulling Grace close.

Through the smoke, a tall form prowled toward them.

"Toren," Sage called out.

Toren's weapon swiveled around, aiming toward Acton. Lasers fired, hitting the chains holding him prisoner, and melting them. Acton guessed that the cyborg's earlier injuries were partly healed, as they weren't slowing him down.

Acton tried to sit up, but his head swam. Sage and Toren appeared, easing him upright.

"The others?" Sage asked.

"On the way," Toren answered. "I swam through the tunnels after you." He looked at Simone and Grace.

"That was *badass*." Grace stared at Toren's weapon. "I want one of those."

There was a faint line of amusement on the cyborg's face.

"Simone, Grace, this is Toren."

The cyborg inclined his head. Suddenly, laser fire rained down on them.

Sage leaped on Acton, but he turned, sliding them off the bench. Toren spun, pulling Simone and Grace to the ground.

"What are you doing?" Acton tried to cover Sage with his body.

"Protecting you," she bit out. "We need to move. Can you walk?"

He nodded and she helped him to his feet. He was

painfully unsteady, unfamiliar dizziness making it hard to focus. Sage caught him before he toppled, wedging herself against his side.

"We can do this," she said firmly.

He was completely in love with Sage McAlister. It was an emotion that just days ago, he didn't know, hadn't wanted, and thought himself incapable of feeling.

Sage had changed all of that.

Nearby, Toren lifted Grace into his arms and grabbed Simone's hand.

They started across the cavern. All around, shouts echoed off the walls and laser fire lit up the smoke.

Acton knew they needed to move fast. The Edull would hunt them down. But he couldn't force any more speed from his battered body.

Suddenly, Simone stopped. She started fiddling with some chemicals that were sitting on a workbench.

"Move," Toren ordered, tugging on her hand.

The woman tossed her tangled hair back, her face serious. "I'll buy us some time."

Grace nodded. "I learned everything from my mom." There was pride in the girl's voice. "If anyone can make the best bombs, it's mom."

Simone stared at Toren. "Get my daughter out of here, cyborg,"

He stared back. "Don't be long. Otherwise I'll come back and find you."

Toren moved over to Acton, sliding an arm around him. With his other arm, Toren kept Grace on his hip.

Together, they hobbled along.

Sage worried her lip, and Acton knew she was concerned about Simone.

Then there was a huge explosion behind them, and they all jolted. Grace's body froze, looking back.

Toren set the girl down. "Keep going." He kept a tight hand on Grace's hand.

The girl's bottom lip trembled, but then she nodded.

They were getting close to the far wall, and Acton could see the entrances to several tunnels. There was another boom, and young Grace's steps faltered once more.

"Mom," she whispered.

Then a spike of pain skewered through Acton's body. His knees failed, and Sage pitched forward, but Toren kept them both upright.

Toren lowered Acton to the ground and Sage knelt beside him.

"Hold on." She checked his shoulder again, patching up his injury.

"Wait here," Toren said. "I'm going back for Simone." He looked at Grace. "Stay here. I will get your mother."

"You promise?" Grace whispered.

"I promise."

Then the cyborg turned, sprinting into the smoke.

Acton sensed Sage and Grace's concern. "Toren always keeps his promises, and is very efficient at his job."

Sage wrapped an arm around Grace. "These House of Rone cyborgs are tough protectors, and they never give up." She looked at Acton. "They are something special."

He let his gaze trace over her face, and then they hunkered down and waited.

Toren

TOREN HAD to use every bit of his enhanced vision to search the smoke for the foolish woman.

Foolish, but courageous. She'd certainly sent the Edull scrambling.

Then he heard a quiet groan.

Spinning, he spotted a slim arm sticking out from under some overturned boxes. His pulse spiked, and he quickly heaved the boxes off her.

She reared up, lifting an arm to fight.

"Simone."

"Oh, it's you." She slumped in relief.

"I said I'd come back for you."

"Grace?"

"With the others."

He pulled Simone up and she cried out, almost collapsing. He caught her, swinging her into his arms. "You're injured."

She wasn't heavy, although he had noted she was tall for an Earth woman, with sleek, toned limbs. There was definite strength to this woman.

She also had a shard of metal embedded in her thigh.

He lowered her to sit on a crate. "I need to remove this."

"Shit." She bit her lip.

He noticed the move, and found himself looking at her pleasantly shaped lips. Giving a slight shake of his

ANNA HACKETT

head, he focused on the situation. "You can do this, Simone."

Her lips trembled. "What's your name again?"

"Toren."

"Toren—" She gripped his wrist.

He felt a strange sizzle at her touch.

"You promise me that you'll get my little girl out of here." Simone's dark eyes looked deep and endless. "No matter what happens."

"I'll get you both out."

"Promise me. She comes first."

"You're both coming to the House of Rone." He gripped her thigh.

Simone swallowed. There was something in her dark, fathomless eyes that he couldn't quite make out. But whatever it was, he felt a strange, answering throb deep in his chest.

His emotional dampeners had to be malfunctioning due to his injuries.

"Okay." She pulled in a breath. "Give me a second and—"

Using his cyborg speed, Toren yanked the shard out. She cried out and pitched forward.

He caught her. "You need to be strong a little bit longer." He pulled the small kit off his belt, withdrew a bandage, and wrapped it around her thigh.

"You could have warned me." She was panting a little.

"It would have made it worse." He finished tying the bandage. "You've survived this long, and now it's time to

184

push through a little more, and get your daughter to safety."

Simone lifted her chin and nodded, the line of her jaw firm.

Earth women—full of grit, that was for sure.

"You'll help me?" Her voice was quiet, barely audible above the din in the cavern.

But he heard her. He rose and held out a hand. "I'm right here."

She took it, their fingers tangling. "No one's been there for me for a really long time." Her voice cracked.

When she wobbled, Toren pulled her closer. "I'm here."

She took a hobbling step, but he scooped her into his arms.

She gasped. "I can't remember the last time someone carried me."

"Then your luck's changed."

Their gazes locked.

"I guess it has," she murmured.

Toren had to force himself to look away from her face, then he started back toward the others.

CHAPTER EIGHTEEN

S age's heart was beating so hard, she was pretty sure she'd have internal bruising. Toren had been gone a long time.

Was Simone okay? Sage chewed on her lip, casting a worried glance at Grace. The little girl was bouncing on her feet, scanning the smoke. *Please be okay.*

Suddenly, Sage spotted a shape in the smoke. Her chest hitched.

It was them.

Toren was running fast, Simone in his arms. He leaped onto a bench, running along it. Then he jumped down, right near them.

Simone had some blood on her face and a bandage around one thigh. When he set her down, she kept the weight off her left foot.

"Mom." Grace ran to her mother and threw her arms around Simone's waist.

"I'm okay, baby girl."

Toren straightened. "We need—"

A small, metal barb flew out of the smoke and hit Toren's arm. It cut into his skin and he grimaced.

Acton frowned. "Tor—"

Electricity lit up, racing over Toren's body. His jaw locked and his body jerked wildly.

"Toren!" Simone took a step closer, throwing an arm out.

"Don't touch him," Acton warned.

Through the smoke, Sage saw more shapes and heard raspy shouting. The Edull were coming.

"Run." Acton spun to Simone. "Get your child and go."

For a second, Simone appeared torn. She looked at Toren, then Grace. Then she grabbed Grace's hand and started running for the tunnels.

Acton looked at Sage. "Go with them."

She shook her head. Fear was a horrible twisting sensation in her chest. Being caught by the Edull again... But there was no way she could leave Acton.

"Don't even bother trying, cyborg. I'm not leaving."

For the first time ever, she heard him mutter a curse. He swept her closer and a second later, Edull surrounded them.

Toren was flat on the ground now, his body twitching.

Sage dug her hands into her thighs. She itched to help him and prayed he was okay.

Behind her, Acton was breathing heavily and leaning on her. He was nowhere near well enough to fight these Edull.

A tall, thin Edull stepped forward. He had blood on

the side of his face, and his pupils were glowing silver in his dark eyes. His mask was askew.

He eyed them dispassionately, then gave a nod of his head.

Several Edull moved forward and grabbed Toren's arms. They started dragging him away.

Several more moved in, yanking Acton and Sage apart.

"No!" she cried.

Arms grabbed Sage roughly, lifting her off her feet. She found herself hefted over a hard shoulder.

She was carried deeper into the cavern, to a part that wasn't burning. When she was set on her feet, she saw both cyborgs had been laid out on benches and tied down.

Swallowing, she tried to control her fear. She was so damn tired of being afraid.

An Edull stooped down, grabbed her wrists, and tied a rope around them. When he yanked the rope tight, she tried to bite him. He slapped her.

Ouch. Wincing, she saw Acton surge up against his bindings.

"I'm okay." She glared at the Edull.

"I want all their enhancements removed," the tall Edull ordered.

Sage pressed her tied hands to her mouth. *No.* She watched the Edull move closer to Acton and Toren. This was a nightmare.

Several Edull started poking at Toren, gripping the metal on his shoulder enhancement. One lifted a tool and opened a panel.

Toren jerked and groaned.

A tear ran down Sage's cheek. Helpless, she watched as they tore parts off Toren's shoulder. The cyborg's body arched and blood ran down his chest.

They ripped his weapon out.

God.

Toren's pained shout echoed in her ears. Sage curled into a ball, looking down at the floor. She heard Acton's groan of pain and knew that they were hurting him too. As she stared at the stone floor, drowning in despair, she spotted a knife.

Someone had clearly dropped it, and it had been forgotten in the chaos. It wasn't too far away from her.

Chest hitching, she started slowly inching closer to it.

She glanced up to assess the situation, and saw the Edull cut into Acton's remaining cybernetic arm. His teeth were clenched and he groaned in agony.

Her chest was so tight. She *had* to help him. She extended her arms, moving closer to the knife.

Boom.

An explosion rocked the cavern around them.

Sage ducked her head as something whizzed past her. More debris flew, and further explosions lit up the space.

Through the flames, she spotted the silhouettes of Simone and Grace. They were both lobbing makeshift grenades.

God. Sage straightened. Nearby, the flames caught something flammable and started spreading. The Edull started shouting.

In all the confusion, Sage grabbed the knife and yanked it close. Awkwardly, she maneuvered the blade between her hands and started cutting through the rope.

The Edull hurting Acton glared at the fire, then turned back to his victim. His dark eyes were narrowed.

The bindings fell off her wrists. With a growl, Sage launched herself upward.

Surprised, the Edull turned and tried to grab her. She threw the knife, just as Acton had taught her, and it hit right in the center of his mask. The blade destroyed the tiny valve.

He staggered back into the bench, making a harsh sound.

She leaned over and clicked the locks on the bindings holding Acton. He sat up, and then quickly slid off the bench. With his cybernetic hand, he grabbed the Edull's neck and lifted the alien off his feet. The alien hissed, then Acton clenched his fingers together.

Sage looked away. The Edull went silent, and Acton dropped him to the ground. More homemade grenades landed nearby.

Boom. Boom. Boom. Crates and scrap metal went flying.

Sage slid an arm around Acton. "I suggest we leave. *Now.*"

The Edull were rushing to either escape or put the fires out.

"I approve of that idea." Acton pulled her in close for a quick kiss.

Then they turned to look at Toren.

The other cyborg was lying motionless on the bench, his arm hanging limply from the side

Sage's gut clenched. *Oh, no.*

ACTON WORKED HARD to block the pain tearing through his body. Sage rushed to Toren, pressing her fingers to his neck.

"He has a pulse." She turned to the Edull's equipment, rummaging through it. She pulled out several items and started staunching the worst of the blood flow from Toren's injuries.

Acton scanned around, trying to calculate the best way to get them out.

"Acton, he's really hurt." Her gaze ran down Acton's body. "You are, too."

"We'll get out."

"I hope Grace and Simone are okay." She cast a glance toward the flames and smoke.

Steeling himself, Acton leaned down and yanked the knife out of the Edull's face. He wiped it off and handed it back to her.

Resolutely, she took it and slid it into her belt.

So tough, his Sage. Steel wrapped in soft, soft skin.

"I'll carry Toren."

Her eyes widened. "You can barely stay upright yourself."

"I'm a cyborg. And we're not leaving him."

"Of course, we aren't."

Acton crouched and, with Sage's help, got Toren over his shoulder. When he rose, he wavered, his vision blurring.

"Dammit, Acton, you can't carry him."

"I will. Let's go."

She pulled out the knife and held it up, and they weaved unsteadily through the cavern. It was slow going. There were still Edull running around, but they were ignoring them. For now.

One thought kept Acton going—he wanted Sage out of here. He needed her to be safe.

"Release the battle bots," a raspy voice screamed across the space.

"That does *not* sound good," Sage muttered.

Acton focused only on the tunnel entrances ahead, and tried to move faster. One foot in front of the other.

But then he heard the clank of metal behind them, and looked back over his shoulder.

Huge bots—twice his size—rolled off several platforms

Acton's gut hardened.

Sage froze. "Oh, fuck."

All the bots had different designs and wielded different weapons. They were enormous creations. The one in the lead had a huge, circular saw at the front that started up, the buzzing noise humming through the cavern. A red light blinked on the front of it.

Another construct rolled closer, a chain hanging from its hands.

Acton also noted that several had organic parts as well.

He grabbed Sage and shoved her behind him. But she pushed forward and stepped in front of him, her chin up.

"I'm *not* a victim." Her voice was confident, fierce.

"I'll fight. For me—" her gaze met Acton's "—and for you. For us."

Sensation—bright, rich, and intense—rocketed through him, and he knew that this was love. It had been missing all his life, but he felt it for Sage.

One of the bots rolled closer, deadly chain swinging.

The one with the saw followed.

Sage ran at the bots, her knife raised.

"Sage!" Acton's blood ran cold. She was so small compared to the robots.

"Come on, you big toasters!" She darted left.

The chain sailed through the air, smashing into the floor. It had missed her, but only by the smallest amount.

Acton tried to call up his cybernetic power, but his remaining arm was just too broken. Shifting, he set Toren down.

Whatever he had left, he'd use it to fight alongside his woman.

Sage ducked again, moving in close to the bot with the saw. As the chain swung again, she dodged, and came so close to the saw, that strands of her hair were cut off.

Acton sucked in a breath. He watched her taunt the chain-wielding bot, wiggling her fingers. The bot swung the chain.

Sage dived out of the way, rolling across the floor. The chain tangled with the saw on the second bot with the harsh grind of metal.

Bouncing back to her feet, Sage grinned. She looked at Acton and winked.

His smart woman.

Acton charged at the tangled battle bots. He punched

his arm into the first bot, denting the metal. He punched the second one, once, twice. The lights on the bot flickered and died.

He left the bots in a crumpled pile and returned to Sage.

Her face was stained with dirt, but she smiled. He yanked her to his chest with his arm.

Then they heard a deep rumble and thump of metal.

They both lifted their heads.

"Oh, no." She stiffened and his arm clenched on her.

A dozen huge battle bots fanned out around them.

SAGE TRIED to pull some air into her lungs. This was bad. *So, so bad.* She bit down on her lip so hard she tasted blood.

They couldn't fight them all. She wrapped her arms around Acton. "I love you, Acton."

His gaze fell on her.

"I always wanted to belong somewhere," she said. "Have someone look at me like I was enough."

He cupped the side of her neck, his gaze intense.

"You gave me that," she whispered. "When I'm with you, I'm not afraid. When you touch me, I get tingles. Every time."

"I will protect you with my last breath. You are not just enough, Sage McAlister. You're everything."

Her throat tightened. How, in the middle of this horrible situation, could she feel such love?

A loud boom echoed above them.

They both swiveled and Sage frowned. It wasn't another explosion. It sounded deeper, lower. She looked up.

Boom. Rocks rained down from the ceiling.

A large slab of rock broke off, rocketing downward. The bots swiveled, agitated. Acton dived on Sage, dragging her to the ground.

Thud. Thud. Thud.

The rocks hit and she looked up, peeking around Acton's arm.

One bot lay crumpled.

Thud.

Something else landed in the center of the bots.

She sucked in a breath. Magnus was crouched, one palm pressed to the stone floor. He lifted his head, his neon eye glowing.

Sage looked up. The other House of Rone cyborgs were plummeting down from the ceiling.

Jax landed beside Magnus with a flap of his cloak, Quinn in his arms.

Mace landed with a boom. Rillian landed, raising his head, a feral glow in his silver eyes. Light glowed along the casino owner's spine.

Mace drew his sword. Magnus' arm lit up, crackling with electricity.

Without a word, the House of Rone cyborgs attacked.

Sage sucked in a breath. *Bad. Ass.*

The sounds of fighting were loud. The bots swiveled and swung their weapons, but ruthlessly, the House of Rone cut them down.

Mace swung his sword, the heated blade cutting

through metal. Rillian was a powerful predator, pinning one bot down so Jax could slam his arm into it, his tattoos flaring with power.

Quinn's staff was a blur. She worked with Magnus to bring down another huge bot.

"We're going to be okay," she murmured.

Acton nodded, and together, they crawled toward Toren.

They rolled him over and she checked his pulse. She frowned. He was alive. Just barely.

There was more rumbling across the cavern, and ice filled her veins. More bots were pouring into the cavern.

No. Her belly sank.

"Screw you, suckers."

The young voice cut through the air, as did a number of whizzing pieces of metal. Several razor-sharp throwing stars cut into one of the battle bots.

Sage spotted Grace standing on a crate, firing some sort of weapon that used throwing stars as ammunition.

A loud rumble, and a large, spider-like bot landed right beside Grace. The girl lost her balance, her arms pinwheeling. The bot lifted a leg to strike at her.

Mace growled and leaped, landing between Grace and the bot. His skin gleamed silver where it had turned into a living shield. With a powerful slash, he cut the bot's leg off.

Grace's eyes widened. "Wow, you're big."

Mace's sword burned red, and he hacked up the bot, leaving it in tiny pieces.

Another bot rolled into view. It had several large cannons on its shoulders.

"Uh-oh." Grace grimaced.

"Magnus," Jax roared. "There are too many. We need to go!"

Sage stared across at the cells. *No.* They couldn't leave these people.

Grace jumped down off the box and held up a device. "I have an idea."

The cyborgs all stiffened.

"What?" Sage asked. "What is it?"

"A *luma* bomb," Acton said. "It disables bots."

"And cyborgs," Grace said grimly. "I found it just now in a crate with some weapons."

Crap. It would take the cyborgs down and leave them defenseless.

Quinn stepped forward and lifted her staff. She met Sage's gaze and Sage lifted her knife with a nod.

Rillian moved closer, the muscles in his arms flexing. He nodded as well.

Magnus took them in, then looked at Grace. "Do it."

The girl threw the bomb like a star baseball pitcher.

It flew into the air and exploded like a mini super-nova—flashes of blues, gold, and pink ignited.

A second later, Acton sagged, a dead weight against Sage. She cried out at the suddenness of it. She couldn't hold him up and lowered him to the floor.

She turned then, and took in the horrible sight of Magnus, Jax, and Mace crumpling like marionettes who'd had their strings cut.

Quinn knelt by Jax, her hand on his head. Her staff was clenched hard in her other hand. She leaned over the cyborgs, hyper-alert.

But as Sage looked around, she saw all the battle bots had been deactivated. Some had simply collapsed into parts, while others sagged. And the last of the Edull were fleeing into the tunnels.

"The Edull have gone," Sage said.

"Cowards," Quinn spat.

"My mom," Grace called. "She's trapped under some rocks."

"I'll help you," Rillian said.

Grace walked off with him. "You're pretty."

"You too," Rillian replied, all charm.

Sage hugged Acton to her. "I'm right here, baby. I'll keep you safe and be here when you wake up."

Moments later, Rillian was back, helping a limping, bleeding Simone.

Silence reigned then, broken only by quiet murmurs from Simone, Grace, and Rillian, and the occasional pop and crackle of small fires still burning.

It felt like a long time, but Sage guessed it was only minutes later, that the cyborgs started to stir.

Except Toren.

Her face pinched with worry, Simone dropped down beside the lifeless cyborg. She reached out and took his hand. Grace plopped herself down immediately beside her mother.

"Sage?"

Acton's voice made her heart thump hard. She cupped his beloved face. It was covered with blood and dirt, and the metal on his cheek was dented. She helped him sit up.

"I love you," she whispered.

He slid his nose along hers. "I love you too."

"You aren't sorry that you feel chaotic emotions now?" she asked.

"Not one bit." He pulled her closer. "Are you still afraid to let me love you?"

She blinked. "You're pretty perceptive for a guy who's only been feeling a short time."

"I don't want you to be afraid, Sage. I'll spend all my days showing you how I feel about you."

"Then no, I'm not afraid anymore."

His cybernetic fingers brushed along her cheekbone. "Thank you for showing me what love is. Thank you for setting it free inside me."

She buried her face in his chest. "Any time, cyborg, any time."

CHAPTER NINETEEN

The bedraggled group made its way through the tunnels.

Acton limped along with Sage and Jax on either side of him. Toren was still unconscious, and being carried by Mace. Simone and Grace walked beside him, casting worried glances at the injured cyborg.

They weren't alone. They'd freed the hostages locked in the Edull cages—or rather, Magnus, Jax, Quinn, and Mace had. The captives walked quietly behind the cyborgs, helping each other along.

"How did you find us?" Acton asked Jax.

"It wasn't easy," Jax replied. "We searched the tunnels for you, trying to estimate where that shark bot might have taken you."

Sage's nose wrinkled. "I don't want to talk about the sharks."

"Our scanners weren't working properly because of the *dantane* and the tunnels are drakking mazes. That's why it took us so long to get to you." Jax glanced at

Magnus. "Magnus finally detected heat signatures below us, so we just smashed down through the rock."

The tunnel they were in angled upward and a moment later, they stepped out into the desert sunlight.

Acton narrowed his eyes against the brightness. Behind him, voices cried out in joy.

"I'm totally going to get sunburned, but I have never been so happy to see the hot sun," Sage said.

The sunlight felt pleasant on Acton's skin. He saw some of the freed captives drop to their knees in the sand, their faces lifted to the sunlight, tears streaming down their cheeks.

"They've been trapped in the dark for so long," Sage murmured.

"They're free now," Acton said.

Rillian stepped forward. "I'll go, get the ship, and return back here. Some of these people are in bad condition, they won't make the journey back to the ship." He no longer looked crisp and elegant, and instead, the predator he was bonded with showed through. He scanned the motley group. "It'll be a tight fit for everyone."

"Some won't come to Kor Magna," Magnus said. "I'll talk with them, and see who wants to come with us, and who will return to their desert villages. I'll ask Corsair to help them."

Rillian nodded and took off at a run, moving fast. His alien symbiont gave him a lot of speed and strength.

Acton sagged, his own energy failing. Sage leaned into him.

"Sit down before you fall down," she said with a huff.

He let her help him to the sand, and nuzzled her hair. "You smell good."

She snorted. "I smell like sweat, blood, and smoke."

"But under all that is you."

Smiling, she rubbed her cheek against his. They sat on the sand, enjoying the sunshine. Magnus crouched beside them.

"How are you holding up?"

"Fine," Acton answered.

Magnus raised a brow, and Acton knew his imperator wasn't convinced.

"There isn't a part of me that doesn't hurt," Acton admitted.

A faint smile crossed Magnus' face. "Avarn will get you sorted out." The imperator's gaze turned to Sage. "You did well down there."

"Thanks. But if I have fight off giant battle bots again, it will be *way* too soon."

"You got the Edull data?" Acton asked.

Magnus nodded. "I spiked into the Edull systems before we left the cavern. Or what was left of them. The fires had destroyed most of them. I downloaded what I could and we'll analyze the information back at the House of Rone. Maxon can help pull it apart and deduce exactly what the Edull are doing."

Acton grunted. "Maxon doesn't help. He yells, complains, and insults."

"I would like to hear you tell him that." Magnus patted Acton's shoulder. "Rest while you can."

The imperator moved away, talking to the survivors.

Acton drifted in and out of consciousness. He was aware of Sage beside him, playing with his hair.

Next thing he knew, a ship appeared in the sky, the sunlight gleaming off its silver hull. It kicked up sand around them as it landed.

Magnus had been right. Some of the captives were from the desert, and didn't want to go to Kor Magna. A small group from nearby villages set off to return to their families.

The rest of the desert dwellers would be dropped off at the Corsair Caravan, while the off-worlders snatched from other planets accepted Magnus' offer of sanctuary at the House of Rone.

Soon, they were all aboard. It was a tight fit, with people sitting not only on the chairs, but on the floor.

Sage fussed around Acton, checking his injuries, and finally, he tumbled her into his lap.

"I could hurt you," she protested.

"Hold still. I just want to hold you."

She stilled, pressing her cheek to his neck. "So, you love me?"

"Yes. Completely."

Her lip quivered. "God, I love you so much."

Acton kissed her, uncaring that people were watching them.

"So, you guys are in love?"

Acton lifted his head and saw Grace smiling at them. Someone, probably Simone, had made a valiant attempt to wipe the girl's grimy face.

"We sure are," Sage replied.

"But, he's like, part robot."

"But all man." Sage pressed a hand to Acton's chest. "He has a heart, and feelings, just like you and me."

"Although, I sometimes need Sage's help to learn about those feelings and understand them," he said.

The girl turned her head, looking at where Toren was laid out on the floor at the back of the ship. "Does he feel?"

Acton eyed his injured friend. "Yes, deep down, I think he does."

Grace smiled. "Good. And if he needs help, I can help him learn about feelings."

Then the young girl headed back to the other cyborg, carefully making her way through the crowded cabin.

Sage shook her head. "That girl is fierce. I can't believe how well she's come through her ordeal." She snuggled into Acton.

He was tired and hurting, but with Sage wrapped under his arm, he'd never felt better.

SAGE WOKE, startled. She'd slept like the dead.

Fighting off fogginess, she shoved at the sheets tangled around her, and pushed her tumbled hair back.

After stopping at the Corsair Caravan and ensuring the survivors were comfortable with Corsair and his people, they'd gotten back to the House of Rone late in the evening. The healers had gone into overdrive to help the survivors and the injured cyborgs.

But Avarn hadn't let Sage stay while he'd worked on

Acton. She'd argued with the older man, but he'd ordered her to get some rest.

Instead, she'd helped Ever and the House of Rone staff sort out the survivors, and get them settled in quarters with clean clothes and food.

Exhausted, she'd managed a quick shower and had lain down for a quick nap. Clearly, she'd crashed out and slept all night.

Morning sunlight streamed through the windows, and her tired brain clicked into gear.

Acton.

She leaped out of bed and raced out of the room. She sprinted down the hall, ignoring that her hair was a tangled mess and she was clad only in her pajamas. She stopped at Acton's room and threw the door open.

No Acton. The bed was untouched.

Claws gripped her belly.

Spinning, she ran down the corridor, headed for Medical. What if something had gone wrong? What if—?

She ran smack into Magnus.

"Oof."

Magnus gripped her arms. "Sage, are you all right?"

"Sorry. Acton?"

The imperator cupped her cheek. It was such an un-Magnus-like action, but Sage suspected he'd learned it because of his love for his mate and daughter. Ever and Asha had taught this dangerous cyborg to feel.

"He's fine," Magnus said. "He came through his treatment perfectly."

Sage shuddered.

"You love him," Magnus said.

"I do. Like crazy."

"You're good for him, Sage."

"And he's good for me. Do you know where he is?"

"The rooftop."

With a wave, Sage ran to the stairs, taking them two at a time.

Her chest was heaving by the time she rushed out onto the rooftop. She spotted him instantly, and her heart settled.

There was her cyborg.

He was standing at the railing near the seating area, looking out across the city. His skin was all healed, his metal gleaming, and a new cybernetic arm was in place of the one that had been taken from him.

Of course, he heard her and turned.

He stood in the sunlight, so strong and straight, and hers.

Sage ran. He opened his arms and she leaped into them.

"You're all right?" she said against his lips.

"Yes."

"I woke up alone, and I was worried."

"I checked on you when Avarn released me from Medical, but you were sleeping deeply. I wanted you to get some more rest."

"Next time, wake me."

He inclined his head. "Very well."

"And I'm moving into your room. We're making it *our* room."

A smile flirted on his lips. "As you wish."

"Be warned, I'm not as tidy as you."

"I don't care."

His lips touched hers and the kiss started soft, but it soon changed. His arms banded around her and she wrapped her legs around his waist. She moaned into his mouth.

Need rocketed through her. She needed to know that he was okay, to prove they were both very much alive.

"Sage." Her name was a groan.

She undulated against him, feeling the growing bulge in his trousers. "Now, Acton." She slid a hand between them and tugged at his waistband. "I need you now."

"Here?"

"Yes."

He took two steps and laid her down on the big pillows under the shade cloths. He knelt over her and she pressed her hands to his skin. She loved the way his breathing quickened. She stroked his chest, nails scratching at his nipples.

She leaned up to press a kiss to his shoulder, where metal met skin.

But he pushed her back down, nudging her legs wider. He tore at her clothes, leaving her naked, then took seconds to remove his own.

Oh, boy, she loved looking at her cyborg.

He cupped her breasts, molding them in his cool hands. Then his hips moved between hers, and a second later, he thrust inside her.

"*Oh.*" Her back arched.

"You feel so right," he said. "Like home."

She wrapped her legs around him, moving with him. "Love me, Acton."

The need was building between them, but he didn't rush. He used long, deep thrusts, like he was savoring every second.

Sage's release was growing inside her, a tangled ball of love and desire. "Acton!"

"Sage." He plunged faster.

She came hard, pleasure swamping her. She clung to him, heard him grunt and his thrusts turned wild.

Sage sobbed through her climax and held her man as his body shuddered. He groaned her name.

CHAPTER TWENTY

Acton leaned against the wall in Magnus's office. Simone sat stiffly on a chair in front of the desk, Grace in her lap. The girl was freshly washed and dressed in clean clothes. Simone held her child close, and Acton wondered if his parents had ever done that to him.

Then Sage stroked a hand down his arm and he smiled at her. It didn't matter what the past had held, now he had everything he'd never known he'd needed right here, wrapped up in one pretty woman from Earth.

"Simone, anything you can tell us would help," Magnus said. "We want to find Bari Batu, and ensure any other humans out there are rescued."

Simone nodded. "I was at Bari Batu. I saw parts of it." She swallowed, stroking her hand down Grace's shiny, black hair. "I was made to work in a huge warehouse of scrap parts for a while. And I spent some time at the battle arena." She shuddered.

The cyborgs sharpened.

"Battle arena?" Magnus asked.

The woman nodded. "It's horrible. A huge, indoor track where they race large robots. They speed around the track fighting until one destroys the other. The crowd places bets."

"*Drak,*" Jax murmured.

"It gets worse," Simone said quietly. "Grace, maybe you should—"

Grace shifted closer to her mother. "No. I'm not a baby, Mom. I saw stuff. I know the Edull are bad."

Simone squeezed her dark eyes closed, then opened them. "The most popular races are the bio-races."

Magnus leaned forward. "Can you explain them to us?"

The woman pulled in a deep breath. "The bots that have biological enhancements."

"Organic parts," Acton said.

Simone nodded. "Stolen from unwilling donors. You saw what they were doing in that cavern."

Sage gasped and trembled. "Every time I think the Edull can't get any worse, they prove me wrong." Acton grabbed her hand and squeezed.

Simone swallowed. "And they also race bots with living beings trapped inside, forced to pilot them."

The cyborgs grumbled and Acton's fingers clenched on Sage's.

"They have to race, or they die." Simone hugged Grace closer. "And the loser doesn't leave the arena alive."

"Drakking sandsuckers," Jax said.

"Crudspawn," Mace spat.

Magnus rose. "We will not let this abomination

continue. I'll talk with Galen and the other imperators. They are all very unhappy with the Edull."

"I glimpsed another crewmember across the battle arena," Simone added.

Acton straightened and heard Sage gasp.

"Bellamy Walsh. Blonde hair cut short, tattoos. I didn't know her well, but I recognized her when I saw her."

Quinn frowned. "I remember her. She was a mechanic on the *Helios* maintenance crew."

Simone nodded.

"That's very helpful, Simone," Magnus said. "We'll ask around if anyone knows about the battle arena. We'll do everything we can to find Bellamy."

"Whatever I can do to help..."

Magnus nodded.

"How's Toren?" Simone asked. "He risked his life to save me and Grace."

Magnus sat down again and leaned back in his chair. Acton sensed the imperator's disquiet. Just weeks ago, he would have missed it, but Sage had changed him.

"Toren's physical wounds are healing," Magnus said.

Simone straightened. "There's a 'but' in there, somewhere."

For a second, Magnus didn't answer. "His internal circuits sustained serious damage."

"And?" A crease formed on Simone's brow. "What does that mean?"

"His emotional dampeners are malfunctioning. He's been hit with wild swings of emotion."

Drak. Acton pressed his lips together. He'd had time

to adjust to feeling more, bit by bit, with Sage. And she'd been beside him, helping him.

What would it feel like to experience emotion in a huge deluge?

"I'll visit him," Simone said.

"Me too," Sage said. "We're all here for him, the same way the House of Rone has been there for us."

"And we'll find Bellamy," Simone said. "She doesn't deserve to be out there, alone and enslaved by the Edull."

Magnus nodded. "I vow that we'll find her. The entire House of Rone is committed to this."

"I'd like to help with the search," Simone said firmly. "I *need* to be a part of it."

"And you may," Magnus said. "But first, you and Grace need to get settled here."

Simone looked prepared to argue, but finally, she looked at her daughter and nodded.

There was a knock at the door, and it opened to reveal Ever, with Nemma standing by her side. The little girl rushed over to Grace.

"Hi, Grace. I came to see if you wanted to come and play."

Grace grinned. "Sure."

"No chemicals," Simone said quietly.

Grace nodded and took the younger girl's hand. The girls rushed off together.

Two girls who'd been through a nightmare, but still saw the good in life.

"Your daughter is very resilient," Acton said.

Simone looked up at him, shadows in her eyes. "I

wish she didn't have to be." Simone rose slowly, as though her bones ached. With a nod, she left the office.

"She needs time," Sage said. "A wise cyborg told me that once."

"Sounds like a very intelligent man," Acton replied.

With a smile, she elbowed him. "Oh, he is. And a fast learner, and good with his hands, and his lips—"

He wrapped an arm around her and pinched her side.

As the others around them laughed and shook their heads, Sage smiled. Looking at her, love glowed inside him, huge and bright. Her nightmare was over. For both of them, the dark and cold were gone, leaving only light and love.

"I WANT YOU TO FIX ME!"

Sage winced at Toren's rage-filled roar.

They were standing in the middle of Medical, and she watched as the cyborg grabbed a stool, spun, and tossed it against the wall.

It crashed down, hitting a cart of medical equipment. Items spilled across the floor.

"Toren." Avarn advanced, hands outstretched, looking resigned.

Toren stood there, his chest heaving, his muscles strained.

"There's nothing wrong with you, Toren," Sage said. "Most people feel like you do."

His hot gaze hit her almost like a physical blow, and she fought the urge to step back.

"All I feel is rage, pain... It's too *much*." He pressed his hands to his head.

"Give it some time," she said calmly. "It'll settle down, and you'll learn to deal with it."

His head jerked up. "I can't function like *this*. I'm not allowed to work."

Avarn stepped closer. "Once your emotions are in control—"

"I don't want to feel!" Toren's hands curled into fists. "I don't want to be like this."

"Toren." Acton's cool voice cut through the tension.

Sage felt a flood of relief at the sight of her man in the doorway.

"What do you want?" Toren snarled.

"I want you to calm down," Acton said.

"You still have dampeners," Toren bit out the words like an accusation.

"Which I don't use now. If I can do it, you can."

Toren's shoulders sagged. He looked broken, beaten.

Then he dropped to his knees and let out a roar of frustration. Sage moved straight to him, wrapping her arms around him.

"You're not alone," she told him. His body vibrated with emotion under her touch.

The doors opened behind Acton, and Toren's head snapped up.

Simone stepped inside.

The woman wore a fitted blue skirt and patterned

white shirt. Her glossy, black hair rested over one slim shoulder.

She stared at him, and his face twisted, different emotions crossing his features.

Simone walked over and Sage stepped back, watching.

What was this? She knew that Simone and Grace had been in to visit Toren a few times over the last few days since their return from the desert.

"You're strong, Toren," Simone said. "You're not just your enhancements. Use that strength now."

They stared at each other—Simone standing, Toren on his knees. Toren made a sound—part pain, part rage—then lunged at Simone.

Acton took a step forward, Sage stiffened, and Avarn moved.

But Toren just wrapped his arms around Simone's waist and buried his face against her belly.

Simone stroked his blond hair. "It's going to be okay."

The damaged cyborg held on like the woman was a lifeline. Sage sensed the storm of emotion in the room ease a little.

Acton took her hand and together, they quietly left Medical.

"He's hurting so badly," she said.

"He needs time to heal and adjust."

"Simone seems to be a calming influence."

He tugged on Sage's hair. "I'm beginning to think that you women from Earth are capable of anything. He'll be fine. We'll make sure of it."

That was the House of Rone. They got on with it and

did what needed to be done, no matter the obstacles in the way. Just like the way they'd rescued, protected, and helped the *Helios* survivors.

The House of Rone took care of their own. They'd help Toren. And Sage suspected the cyborg would have a little extra help from a new pair of residents as well.

Suddenly, Acton pulled Sage down an empty corridor, and nudged her against the wall. His big body pressed into hers, his mouth on her neck. He hit a sensitive spot, and she arched into him

"You feeling a little frisky, cyborg?"

"I can't get enough of my mate."

Mate. The word made her heart skip a beat.

Of course, he sensed it, and raised his head. "You're mine, Sage. I don't care what label we use. Mate, wife, partner. You're mine, and I'm yours. Forever."

She could barely breathe. "Forever."

"You're the most important thing in my world."

Her heart filled to bursting. She'd dreamed of a prince or a knight who'd want her more than anything else. But she'd never imagined in her wildest dreams that her knight would be an alien cyborg with metal arms and a part metal face.

She reached up, stroking that metal cheek. His hands drifted lower, then gripped her skirt, sliding it up her legs.

She licked her lips. "Acton, we can't fool around here."

"We did on the rooftop."

"That was more private."

"I can assure you that this isn't a well-used corridor. The statistical chances of someone catching us are—"

She laughed and pulled away. "I do love it when you talk cyborg. It makes my panties wet."

His eyes flared with heat.

Sage wriggled out of his arms. "I think our nice, big bed would work better for the things I want to do to you." She turned and ran. "Catch me if you can!"

She heard his heavy steps following her.

"You will never get away from me," he growled. "Wherever you run, I'll follow."

Which was good, because she didn't want to ever get away from this man.

As his cybernetic arms lifted her off her feet, and his mouth closed over hers, Sage knew that her cyborg would be there right beside her. Always.

I hope you enjoyed Sage and Acton's story!

Galactic Gladiators: House of Rone continues with PALADIN, the story of injured cyborg Toren and human scientist Simone. Coming in 2020.

Did you miss the *House of Rone* novella, DARK GUARD, starring cyborg Zaden, alien survivor Calla, and a nosy cyborg cat? Available as part of the Pets in Space 4 anthology.

If you're interested in learning more about the House of Galen gladiators and the strong, smart women from Earth they helped rescue or Magnus and Ever's story, then check out Galactic Gladiators.

For more action-packed romance, read on for a preview of the first chapter of *Edge of Eon,* the first book in my best-selling Eon Warriors series.

Don't miss out! For updates about new releases, action romance info, free books, and other fun stuff, sign up for my VIP mailing list and get your *free box set* containing three action-packed romances.

Visit here to get started: www.annahackettbooks.com

FREE BOX SET DOWNLOAD

JOIN THE ACTION-PACKED ADVENTURE!

PREVIEW: EDGE OF EON

She shifted on the chair, causing the chains binding her hands to clank together. Eve Traynor snorted. The wrist and ankle restraints were overkill. She was on a low-orbit prison circling Earth. Where the fuck did they think she was going to go?

Eve shifted her shoulders to try to ease the tension

from having her hands tied behind her back. For the millionth time, she studied her surroundings. The medium-sized room was empty, except for her chair. Everything from the floor to the ceiling was dull-gray metal. All of the Citadel Prison was drab and sparse. She'd learned every boring inch of it the last few months.

One wide window provided the only break in the otherwise uniform space. Outside, she caught a tantalizing glimpse of the blue-green orb of Earth below.

Her gut clenched and she drank in the sight of her home. Five months she'd been locked away in this prison. Five months since her life had imploded.

She automatically thought of her sisters. She sucked in a deep breath. She hated everything they'd had to go through because of what had happened. Hell, she thought of her mom as well, even though their last contact had been the day after Eve had been imprisoned. Her mom had left Eve a drunken, scathing message.

The door to the room opened, and Eve lifted her chin and braced.

When she saw the dark-blue Space Corps uniform, she stiffened. When she saw the row of stars on the lapel, she gritted her teeth.

Admiral Linda Barber stepped into the room, accompanied by a female prison guard. The admiral's hair was its usual sleek bob of highlighted, ash-blonde hair. Her brown eyes were steady.

Eve looked at the guard. "Take me back to my cell."

The admiral lifted a hand. "Please leave us."

The guard hesitated. "That's against protocol, ma'am—"

"It'll be fine." The admiral's stern voice said she was giving an order, not making a request.

The guard hesitated again, then ducked through the door. It clicked closed behind her.

Eve sniffed. "Say what you have to say and leave."

Admiral Barber sighed, taking a few steps closer. "I know you're angry. You have a right to be—"

"You think?" Eve sucked back the rush of molten anger. "I got tossed under the fucking starship to save a mama's boy. A mama's boy who had no right to be in command of one of Space Corps' vessels."

Shit. Eve wanted to pummel something. Preferably the face of Robert J. Hathaway—golden son of Rear-Admiral Elisabeth Hathaway. A man who, because of family connections, was given captaincy of the *Orion*, even though he lacked the intelligence and experience needed to lead it.

Meanwhile, Eve—a Space Corps veteran—had worked her ass off during her career in the Corps, and had been promised her own ship, only to be denied her chance. Instead, she'd been assigned as Hathaway's second-in-command. To be a glorified babysitter, and to actually run the ship, just without the title and the pay raise.

She'd swallowed it. Swallowed Hathaway's incompetence and blowhard bullshit. Until he'd fucked up. Big-time.

"The Haumea Incident was regrettable," Barber said.

Eve snorted. "Mostly for the people who died. And definitely for me, since I'm the one shackled to a chair in the Citadel. Meanwhile, I assume Bobby Hathaway is still a dedicated Space Corps employee."

"He's no longer a captain of a ship. And he never will be again."

"Right. Mommy got him a cushy desk job back at Space Corps Headquarters."

The silence was deafening and it made Eve want to kick something.

"I'm sorry, Eve. We all know what happened wasn't right."

Eve jerked on her chains and they clanked against the chair. "And you let it happen. All of Space Corps leadership did, to appease Mommy Hathaway. I dedicated my life to the Corps, and you all screwed me over for an admiral's incompetent son. I got sentenced to prison for *his* mistakes." Stomach turning in vicious circles, Eve looked at the floor, sucking in air. She stared at the soft booties on her feet. Damned inmate footwear. She wasn't even allowed proper fucking shoes.

Admiral Barber moved to her side. "I'm here to offer you a chance at freedom."

Gaze narrowing, Eve looked up. Barber looked... nervous. Eve had never seen the self-assured woman nervous before.

"There's a mission. If you complete it, you'll be released from prison."

Interesting. "And reinstated? With a full pardon?"

Barber's lips pursed and her face looked pinched. "We can negotiate."

So, no. "Screw your offer." Eve would prefer to rot in her cell, rather than help the Space Corps.

The admiral moved in front of her, her low-heeled pumps echoing on the floor. "Eve, the fate of the world depends on this mission."

Barber's serious tone sent a shiver skating down Eve's spine. She met the woman's brown eyes.

"The Kantos are gathering their forces just beyond the boundary at Station Omega V."

Fuck. The Kantos. The insectoid alien race had been nipping at Earth for years. Their humanoid-insectoid soldiers were the brains of the operation, but they encompassed all manner of ugly, insect-like beasts as well.

With the invention of zero-point drives several decades ago, Earth's abilities for space exploration had exploded. Then, thirty years ago, they'd made first contact with an alien species—the Eon.

The Eon shared a common ancestor with the humans of Earth. They were bigger and broader, with a few differing organs, but generally human-looking. They had larger lungs, a stronger, bigger heart, and a more efficiently-designed digestion system. This gave them increased strength and stamina, which in turn made them excellent warriors. Unfortunately, they also wanted nothing to do with Earth and its inferior Terrans.

The Eon, and their fearsome warriors and warships, stayed inside their own space and had banned Terrans from crossing their boundaries.

Then, twenty years ago, the first unfortunate and bloody meeting with the Kantos had occurred.

Since then, the Kantos had returned repeatedly to nip at the Terran borders—attacking ships, space stations, and colonies.

But it had become obvious in the last year or so that the Kantos had something bigger planned. The Haumea Incident had made that crystal clear.

The Kantos wanted Earth. There were to be no treaties, alliances, or negotiations. They wanted to descend like locusts and decimate everything—all the planet's resources, and most of all, the humans.

Yes, the Kantos wanted to freaking use humans as a food source. Eve suppressed a shudder.

"And?" she said.

"We have to do whatever it takes to save our planet."

Eve tilted her head. "The Eon."

Admiral Barber smiled. "You were always sharp, Eve. Yes, the Eon are the only ones with the numbers, the technology, and the capability to help us repel the Kantos."

"Except they want nothing to do with us." No one had seen or spoken with an Eon for three decades.

"Desperate times call for desperate measures."

Okay, Eve felt that shiver again. She felt like she was standing on the edge of a platform, about to be shoved under the starship again.

"What's the mission?" she asked carefully.

"We want you to abduct War Commander Davion Thann-Eon."

Holy fuck. Eve's chest clenched so tight she couldn't even draw a breath. Then the air rushed into her lungs, and she threw her head back and laughed. Tears ran down her face.

"You're kidding."

But the admiral wasn't laughing.

Eve shook her head. "That's a fucking suicide mission. You want me to abduct the deadliest, most decorated Eon war commander who controls the largest, most destructive Eon warship in their fleet?"

"Yes."

"No."

"Eve, you have a record of making…risky decisions."

Eve shook her head. "I always calculate the risks."

"Yes, but you use a higher margin of error than the rest of us."

"I've always completed my missions successfully." The Haumea Incident excluded, since that was Bobby's brilliant screw-up.

"Yes. That's why we know if anyone has a chance of making this mission a success, it's you."

"I may as well take out a blaster and shoot myself right now. One, I'll never make it into Eon space, let alone aboard the *Desteron*."

Since the initial encounter, they'd collected whatever intel they could on the Eon. Eve had seen secret schematics of that warship. And she had to admit, the thought of being aboard that ship left her a little damp between her thighs. She loved space and flying, and the big, sleek warship was something straight out of her fantasies.

"We have an experimental, top-of-the-line stealth ship for you to use," the admiral said.

Eve carried on like the woman hadn't spoken. "And two, even if I got close to the war commander, he's bigger and stronger than me, not to mention bonded to a fucking deadly alien symbiont that gives him added strength and the ability to create organic armor and weapons with a single thought. I'd be dead in seconds."

"We recovered a...substance that is able to contain the symbiont the Eon use."

Eve narrowed her eyes. "Recovered from where?"

Admiral Barber cleared her throat. "From the wreck of a Kantos ship. It was clearly tech they were developing to use against the Eon."

Shit. "So I'm to abduct the war commander, and then further enrage him by neutralizing his symbiont."

"We believe the containment is temporary, and there is an antidote."

Eve shook her head. "This is beyond insane."

"For the fate of humanity, we have to try."

"*Talk* to them," Eve said. "Use some diplomacy."

"We tried. They refused all contact."

Because humans were simply ants to the Eon. Small, insignificant, an annoyance.

Although, truth be told, humanity only had itself to blame. By all accounts, Terrans hadn't behaved very well at first contact. The meetings with the Eon had turned into blustering threats, different countries trying to make alliances with the aliens while happily stabbing each other in the back.

Now Earth wanted to abduct an Eon war commander. No, not a war commander, *the* war commander. So dumb. She wished she had a hand free so she could slap it over her eyes.

"Find another sacrificial lamb."

The admiral was silent for a long moment. "If you

won't do it for yourself or for humanity, then do it for your sisters."

Eve's blood chilled and she cocked her head. "What's this got to do with my sisters?"

"They've made a lot of noise about your imprisonment. Agitating for your freedom."

Eve breathed through her nose. God, she loved her sisters. Still, she didn't know whether to be pleased or pissed. "And?"

"Your sister has shared some classified information with the press about the Haumea Incident."

Eve fought back a laugh. Lara wasn't shy about sharing her thoughts about this entire screwed-up situation. Eve's older sister was a badass Space Corps special forces marine. Lara wouldn't hesitate to take down anyone who pissed her off, the Space Corps included.

"And she had access to information she should not have had access to, meaning your other sister has done some...creative hacking."

Dammit. The rush of love was mixed with some annoyance. Sweet, geeky Wren had a giant, super-smart brain. She was a computer-systems engineer for some company with cutting-edge technology in Japan. It helped keep her baby sister's big brain busy, because Wren hadn't found a computer she couldn't hack.

"Plenty of people are unhappy with what your sisters have been stirring up," Barber continued.

Eve stiffened. She didn't like where this was going.

"I've tried to run interference—"

"Admiral—"

Barber held up a hand. "I can't keep protecting them,

Eve. I've been trying, but some of this is even above my pay grade. If you don't do this mission, powers outside of my control will go after them. They'll both end up in a cell right alongside yours until the Kantos arrive and blow this prison out of the sky."

Her jaw tight, Eve's brain turned all the information over. *Fucking fuck.*

"Eve, if there is anyone who has a chance of succeeding on this mission, it's you."

Eve stayed silent.

Barber stepped closer. "I don't care if you do it for yourself, the billions of people of Earth, or your sisters—"

"I'll do it." The words shot out of Eve, harsh and angry.

She'd do it—abduct the scariest alien war commander in the galaxy—for all the reasons the admiral listed—to clear her name, for her freedom, to save the world, and for the sisters she loved.

Honestly, it didn't matter anyway, because the odds of her succeeding and coming back alive were zero.

EVE LEFT THE STARSHIP GYM, towel around her neck, and her muscles warm and limber from her workout.

God, it was nice to work out when it suited her. On the Citadel Prison, exercise time was strictly scheduled, monitored, and timed.

Two crew members came into view, heading down the hall toward her. As soon as the uniformed men spotted her, they looked at the floor and passed her quickly.

Eve rolled her eyes. Well, she wasn't aboard the *Polaris* to make friends, and she had to admit, she had a pretty notorious reputation. She'd never been one to blindly follow the rules, plus there was the Haumea Incident and her imprisonment. And her family were infamous in the Space Corps. Her father had been a space marine, killed in action in one of the early Kantos encounters. Her mom had been a decorated Space Corps member, but after Eve's dad had died, her mom had started drinking. It had deteriorated until she'd gone off the rails. She'd done it quite publicly, blaming the Space Corps for her husband's death. In the process, she'd forgotten she had three young, grieving girls.

Yep, Eve was well aware that the people you cared for most either left you, or let you down. The employer you worked your ass off for treated you like shit. The only two people in the galaxy that didn't apply to were her sisters.

Eve pushed thoughts of her parents away. Instead, she scanned the starship. The *Polaris* was a good ship. A mid-size cruiser, she was designed for exploration, but well-armed as well. Eve guessed they'd be heading out beyond Neptune about now.

The plan was for the *Polaris* to take her to the edge of Eon space, where she'd take a tiny, two-person stealth ship, sneak up to the *Desteron*, then steal onboard.

Piece of cake. She rolled her eyes.

Back in her small cabin, she took a quick shower, dressed, and then headed to the ops room. It was a small room close to the bridge that the ship's captain had made available to her.

She stepped inside, and all the screens flickered to life. A light table stood in the center of the room, and everything was filled with every scrap of intel that the Space Corps had on the Eon Empire, their warriors, the *Desteron*, and War Commander Thann-Eon.

It was more than she'd guessed. A lot of it had been classified. There was fascinating intel on the four Eon homeworld planets—Eon, Jad, Felis, and Ath. Each Eon warrior carried their homeworld in their name, along with their clan names. The war commander hailed from the planet Eon, and Thann was a clan known as a warrior clan.

Eve swiped her fingers across the light table and studied pictures of the *Desteron*. They were a few years old and taken from a great distance, but that didn't hide the warship's power.

It was fearsome. Black, sleek, and impressive. It was built for speed and stealth, but also power. It had to be packed with weapons beyond their imagination.

She touched the screen again and slid the image to the side. Another image appeared—the only known picture of War Commander Thann-Eon.

Jesus. The man packed a punch. All Eon warriors looked alike—big, broad-shouldered, muscular. They all had longish hair—not quite reaching the shoulders, but not cut short, either. Their hair usually ranged from dark brown to a tawny, golden-brown. There was no black or blond hair among the Eon. Their skin color ranged from dark-brown to light-brown, as well.

Before first contact had gone sour, both sides had done some DNA testing, and confirmed the Eon and Terrans shared an ancestor.

The war commander was wearing a pitch-black, sleeveless uniform. He was tall, built, with long legs and powerful thighs. He was exactly the kind of man you expected to stride onto a battlefield, pull a sword, and slaughter everyone. He had a strong face, one that shouted power. Eve stroked a finger over the image. He had a square jaw, a straight, almost aggressive nose, and a well-formed brow. His eyes were as dark as space, but shot through with intriguing threads of blue.

"It's you and me, War Commander." If he didn't kill her, first.

Suddenly, sirens blared.

Eve didn't stop to think. She slammed out of the ops room and sprinted onto the bridge.

Inside, the large room was a flurry of activity.

Captain Chen stood in the center of the space, barking orders at his crew.

Her heart contracted. God, she'd missed this so much. The vibration of the ship beneath her feet, her team around her, even the scent of recycled starship air.

"You shouldn't be in here," a sharp voice snapped.

Eve turned, locking gazes with the stocky, bearded XO. Sub-Captain Porter wasn't a fan of hers.

"Leave her," Captain Chen told his second-in-command. "She's seen more Kantos ships than all of us combined."

The captain looked back at his team. "Shields up."

Eve studied the screen and the Kantos ship approaching.

It looked like a bug. It had large, outstretched legs, and a bulky, segmented, central fuselage. It wasn't the biggest ship she'd seen, but it wasn't small, either. It was probably out on some intel mission.

"Sir," a female voice called out. "We're getting a distress call from the *Panama*, a cargo ship en route to Nightingale Space Station. They're under attack from a swarm of small Kantos ships."

Eve sucked in a breath, her hand curling into a fist. This was a usual Kantos tactic. They would overwhelm a ship with their small swarm ships. It had ugly memories of the Haumea Incident stabbing at her.

"Open the comms channel," the captain ordered.

"Please...help us." A harried man's voice came over the distorted comm line. "...can't hold out much...thirty-seven crew onboard...we are..."

Suddenly, a huge explosion of light flared in the distance.

Eve's shoulders sagged. The cargo ship was gone.

"Goddammit," the XO bit out.

The front legs of the larger Kantos ship in front of them started to glow orange.

"They're going to fire," Eve said.

The captain straightened. "Evasive maneuvers."

His crew raced to obey the orders, the *Polaris* veering suddenly to the right.

"The swarm ships will be on their way back." Eve knew the Kantos loved to swarm like locusts.

"Release the tridents," the captain said.

Good. Eve watched the small, triple-pronged space mines rain out the side of the ship. They'd be a dangerous minefield for the Kantos swarm.

The main Kantos ship swung around.

"They're locking weapons," someone shouted.

Eve fought the need to shout out orders and offer the captain advice. Last time she'd done that, she'd ended up in shackles.

The blast hit the *Polaris*, the shields lighting up from the impact. The ship shuddered.

"Shields holding, but depleting," another crew member called out.

"Sub-Captain Traynor?" The captain's dark gaze met hers.

Something loosened in her chest. "It's a raider-class cruiser, Captain. You're smaller and more maneuverable. You need to circle around it, spray it with laser fire. Its weak spots are on the sides. Sustained laser fire will eventually tear it open. You also need to avoid the legs."

"Fly circles around it?" a young man at a console said. "That's crazy."

Eve eyed the lead pilot. "You up for this?"

The man swallowed. "I don't think I can..."

"Sure you can, if you want us to survive this."

"Walker, do it," the captain barked.

The pilot pulled in a breath and the *Polaris* surged forward. They rounded the Kantos ship. Up close, the bronze-brown hull looked just like the carapace of an insect. One of the legs swung up, but Walker had quick reflexes.

"Fire," Eve said.

The weapons officer started firing. Laser fire hit the Kantos ship in a pretty row of orange.

"Keep going," Eve urged.

They circled the ship, firing non-stop.

Eve crossed her arms over her chest. Everything in her was still, but alive, filled with energy. She'd always known she was born to stand on the bridge of a starship.

"More," she urged. "Keep firing."

"Swarm ships incoming," a crew member yelled.

"Hold," Eve said calmly. "Trust the mines." She eyed the perspiring weapons officer. "What's your name, Lieutenant?"

"Law, ma'am. Lieutenant Miriam Law."

"You're doing fine, Law. Ignore the swarm ships and keep firing on the cruiser."

The swarm ships rushed closer, then hit the field of mines. Eve saw the explosions, like brightly colored pops of fireworks.

The lasers kept cutting into the hull of the larger Kantos ship. She watched the ship's engines fire. They were going to try and make a run for it.

"Bring us around, Walker. Fire everything you have, Law."

They swung around to face the side of the Kantos ship straight on. The laser ripped into the hull.

There was a blinding flash of light, and startled exclamations filled the bridge. She squinted until the light faded away.

On the screen, the Kantos ship broke up into pieces.

Captain Chen released a breath. "Thank you, Sub-Captain."

Eve inclined her head. She glanced at the silent crew. "Good flying, Walker. And excellent shooting, Law."

But she looked back at the screen, at the debris hanging in space and the last of the swarm ships retreating.

They'd keep coming. No matter what. It was ingrained in the Kantos to destroy.

They had to be stopped.

Eon Warriors

Edge of Eon
Touch of Eon
Heart of Eon
Kiss of Eon
Mark of Eon (coming soon)
Also Available as Audiobooks!

Heart of Eon

Kiss of Eon

Also Available as Audiobooks!

Galactic Gladiators: House of Rone

Sentinel

Defender

Also Available as Audiobooks!

Galactic Gladiators

Gladiator

Warrior

Hero

Protector

Champion

Barbarian

Beast

Rogue

Guardian

Cyborg

Imperator

Hunter

Also Available as Audiobooks!

Hell Squad

Marcus

Cruz

Gabe

Reed

Roth

Noah

Shaw

Holmes

Niko

Finn

Theron

Hemi

Ash

Levi

Manu

Griff

Dom

Also Available as Audiobooks!

The Anomaly Series

Time Thief

Mind Raider

Soul Stealer

Salvation

Anomaly Series Box Set

The Phoenix Adventures

Among Galactic Ruins

At Star's End

In the Devil's Nebula

On a Rogue Planet

Beneath a Trojan Moon

Beyond Galaxy's Edge

On a Cyborg Planet

Return to Dark Earth

On a Barbarian World

Lost in Barbarian Space

Through Uncharted Space

Crashed on an Ice World

Perma Series

Winter Fusion

A Galactic Holiday

Warriors of the Wind

Tempest

Storm & Seduction

Fury & Darkness

Standalone Titles

Savage Dragon

Hunter's Surrender

One Night with the Wolf

For more information visit AnnaHackettBooks.com

ABOUT THE AUTHOR

I'm a USA Today bestselling author and I'm passionate about *action romance*. I love stories that combine the thrill of falling in love with the excitement of action, danger and adventure. I'm a sucker for that moment when the team is walking in slow motion, shoulder-to-shoulder heading off into battle. I write about people overcoming unbeatable odds and achieving seemingly impossible goals. I like to believe it's possible for all of us to do the same.

My books are mixture of action, adventure and sexy romance and they're recommended for anyone who enjoys fast-paced stories where the boy wins the girl at the end (or sometimes the girl wins the boy!)

For release dates, action romance info, free books, and other fun stuff, sign up for the latest news here:

Website: www.annahackettbooks.com